Jeanette-

xoxo

Victor A.

WALK OF SHAME 2ND GENERATION BOOK THREE

VICTORIA ASHLEY

Kash
Copyright © 2017 Victoria Ashley

Cover Artist:
CT Cover Creations

Photographer:
Eric Battershell Photography

Cover Model:
Drew Truckle

Interior Design & Formatting:
Christine Borgford, Type A Formatting

KASH

I SHOW UP AT THE address I was given, to see Stone, Myles and Colt are already waiting outside for me, dressed in their fitted suits.

Stone tugs on his tie and checks out my hoodie and jeans as if there's something wrong with the way I look.

"Dude . . ." he pushes my hood back. "Where's your suit? I thought we all agreed to dress up and shit. You look like a homeless stripper."

I unzip my hoodie and walk past him with a grin, pulling it open so he can see my ripped-up t-shirt. Then I zip it back up when he flicks a rolled-up dollar bill at my head and scowls.

He knows I said no repeatedly to dressing up, but he ended the call assuming I'd listen anyway. "Nah, you three agreed on a suit. My ass got called out of bed in the middle of the night to be here so I threw on the first thing I saw."

Gotta stand out somehow when it comes to making money and I've learned women like a little mystery.

Colt looks down at his black vest, before unbuttoning it and rolling up the sleeves of his button down. "Shit. I knew we were overdressed." He tosses his jacket at his motorcycle and scowls. "I'm making sure this shit comes off fast. I look awkward as hell."

I have to admit it's funny as shit seeing Colt dressed up. We're all used to his t-shirts, jeans and beanies.

Just wanting to get the night over with, I ignore the idiots and walk up to the door, about ready to knock.

As I stand here with my fist in the air, I begin to think we're at the wrong house, because it's completely quiet. No signs of people talking or even a TV playing in the background.

That's extremely odd.

These kinds of parties are always filled with wild women, that can't sit still or wait for us to arrive. There's no way anyone inside that house is waiting on us.

I just hope like hell I didn't get dragged out of bed for nothing. I might just have to choke Stone then, due to the fact that I have to be up in less than six hours.

Looking around, Stone loosens his collar and stands back as if he's checking out the address. "This is it. Just walk in and start shaking your dick. They're probably waiting on us to get the party started."

I'm just about to open the door–thinking maybe they are just waiting on us–when a whistle comes from across the street, causing me to turn around.

"Over here, boys!" Some chick with long, curly blonde hair crosses her arms and leans against the closed door, watching us as we cross the street. "My friend gets confused about her address when she drinks. Either that or she just likes to screw with people. I haven't figured it out yet."

I stop in front of her and take a few moments to check her out in her tight jeans and loose fitting shirt that hangs off one shoulder.

She looks unamused by our arrival as if she's only here because she was forced to be. The concentration on her face as she looks down at her phone and types fast, tells me there's somewhere else she'd rather be.

"Just go in and start doing whatever it is that you do. The others are eagerly awaiting your arrival. They've been talking firm bodies and tight butts all night. Said you guys are the real deal. Better prove them right." Without looking up, she moves away from the door, allowing us access to the house.

Stone and the newest members of the club, step inside without hesitation, while I take this moment to breathe in the coolness of the night air and wake up a bit more.

Screams of excitement instantly fill the house, before music blares over the speakers, making it clear the party has started without me.

Good, let them wear the women down a little first. My ass is still half-asleep and to be honest, I'm a little intrigued by the sexy little blonde next to me.

"Why aren't you inside with the others? Groping half-naked men isn't your thing?" I question with a lifted brow.

She looks up from her phone and gives me a half smile. "Only on some nights and tonight isn't one of them."

I laugh at her response and pull out a cigarette, lighting it up and taking a long drag.

I need to be more awake before going inside and I have a feeling she's just the one to get me in the mood.

Out of the corner of my eye, I notice her checking me out, but I pretend I don't notice.

"You going to keep that hood up all night? Not quite as handsome as the other guys? Is that it?" She laughs. "Don't be shy. I'm sure you have a great body that will do the trick just fine for my friends."

I smile and take another drag off my cigarette, before slowly exhaling. As much as she doesn't want to admit it, she's desperate to see what's under this hood and probably even my jeans.

Leaning against the porch railing, I push my hood back and smirk as her eyes wander over my face, doing a double take, before finally stopping on my lips.

She swallows and then clears her throat, trying to hide the fact she's surprised by what she sees. "You better get inside with the others. Joni will notice she paid for four guys and only has three actually earning their pay." Her eyes gloss over, focusing on my lips, and her breathing quickens. "I need a drink," she mutters.

I lift a brow and watch as she pulls the screen door open and disappears inside.

After I finish my cigarette, I pull my hood back up and enter the house, hoping I can catch her attention once I start my routine.

Walking through the living room, I notice a lot of heads turn my way, eyes watching me as if they can't wait to see what's under this mysterious fabric.

One girl even walks away from Myles in attempt to check me out.

I walk slowly, ignoring them all, letting my eyes seek out the sassy blonde from outside.

She's in the kitchen pouring a drink, but looks over when a few of her friends grab me and pull me back into the living room.

I stand with a confident smile as they start to grab at my hoodie, unzipping it and checking me out as they rip it from my arms.

Hands grope at my chest, lifting at my shirt as I begin to

move my hips to Ride by *Chase Rice*.

The sassy blonde smirks from the kitchen, watching the other girls take advantage of me as if she finds it to be funny.

This has me smiling.

She's pretending as if she's only watching for the amusement of me being attacked, but the look in her curious green eyes gives away the truth of why she hasn't turned away yet.

I'm guessing she wants to see me naked just as badly as they do. She just doesn't want to be the one to *get* me naked.

Keeping my eyes on her, I bend one of the girls over, place my hand on her lower back and grind my hips against her ass.

I grind slow and seductive, before giving her one hard thrust, almost knocking her over.

She turns back to look at me, her eyes filled with need, before she lays down on her back and waves me over with her finger, wanting more of what I've got to offer.

Standing above the brunette, I slowly pull my shirt over my head, before tossing it aside and dropping down to the ground, rolling my body above hers and rubbing my face over her neck.

Money flies at me as I place her legs over my shoulders and lift her body up, thrusting against her, while on my knees.

After a few seconds, I gently place her down to her back again, before jumping to my feet and reaching for the closest girl next to me, flipping her upside down so my cock is grinding against her face.

Slowly turning around with the girl in my arms, I glance into the kitchen to see the sexy little blonde's eyes on me. As soon as our eyes meet, she turns away and goes back to typing on her phone as if she was never watching in the first place.

Why the hell does that make me want to get to her even more?

Growling, I slap the girl's ass that's in my arms, before flipping her over and setting her back down to her feet.

Cracking my neck, I reach for the button of my jeans, causing desperate screams from all around the room. A sound I used to love, but have grown a bit tired of over the months.

But still, I'm here to do a job and that's exactly what I'll do.

I lick my bottom lip, before slipping my hand inside my jeans and running it over my erection, while slowly letting my pants fall lower with each move of my hips.

My eyes are still on the sassy blonde in the kitchen when she looks up again to see what I'm doing.

Catching her off guard, I slide across the floor on my knees, grab her ass and lift her up so her legs are wrapped around my neck.

Her hands grip at my hair for support as I stand to my feet and walk her over to the wall, pressing her back against it.

I'm not gonna lie, having her in this position has me so damn hard and wanting nothing more than for her body to be pressed against mine.

"Fuck it." I growl against her pussy before biting her inner thigh.

Moving to the music, I grab her legs and lower her down my body, until they're wrapped around my waist now, my dick pressed against her heat.

She says something that the music drowns out, while I hold her up with my hips, pinning her arms against the wall.

I move against her sexy body, while thrusting her up the wall with my erection pressed between her legs.

Fuck, this is extremely hot, making me wish there was nothing between our bodies.

I let out a small growl, enjoying it as she tugs on my hair and squeezes me with her thighs, moving her body perfectly against mine.

She shows enjoyment for a few short minutes, getting lost

in the moment, before dropping her legs to the ground and then pushing at my chest, as I release her arms.

"I'm not here for the entertainment. I'm here for my friend. Find someone else to fuck against the wall." She runs her hands through her hair, looking extremely frustrated with herself. "Shit. I need to go."

I stand in the middle of the room sweaty as fuck, trying to catch my breath as I watch her walk out the front door and leave.

My stomach drops, hating the fact that I pushed her to leave, when apparently all she wanted to do was mind her own business.

Quickly, I walk toward the door, wanting to catch her, but stop when I get blocked in by a group of screaming women, wanting a show.

One of the girls runs her hand over my arm, pulling my attention away from the door. "Don't mind her. Eden's been spending most of her time at a construction site with dirty men lately. Doesn't get out much. She forgets what *fun* is sometimes." The tall brunette grabs my hand and starts pulling me to the other side of the room where a group of women are standing in a circle. "Let's keep this party rocking and rolling, baby. I paid good money for you fine ass men to take your clothes off. I want my floor littered with items of your clothing."

I glance at the door one last time, before looking around me to see the other guys practically naked by this point. All except Stone who refuses to lose his pants at private parties now.

Usually, I'd be having the time of my life, covered in chocolate or whipped cream by now.

But damn . . . this party seems a lot less fun without the sassy blonde watching me.

A couple hours later I'm pulling up outside my house, completely exhausted and ready for bed, again.

My roommate, Colt, won't be home for a few more hours, since he decided to stay and give Joni a private dance, now that the party has ended.

So, I'm stripping out of these sweaty clothes and my ass is crashing on the couch. My bed seems entirely too far away right now.

I'm exhausted.

At least, I think I'm crashing out. Walking up to the porch to see Sara and her girlfriend Kendal, tells me otherwise.

Sara instantly grabs my keys out of my hand and unlocks the door with a wicked smile. "I thought we'd never catch your ass."

I smirk as she pushes me through the door and her girlfriend follows behind. "Yeah, well I'm a busy guy. What can I say?"

Before I know it, I'm slammed against the closed door, by both Sara and Kendal, their hands roaming over my hard body.

Closing my eyes, I lean my head back and just enjoy the feel of their mouths on me. Occasionally, Sara and her girlfriend get an urge for dick, and they want to make sure they get it from a guy they both feel comfortable with.

Over the last few weeks, it's been me. So, I let them use my body any way they please.

Within minutes, I'm completely stripped down and Sara is guiding Kendal's head as her mouth wraps around my cock.

It feels fucking fantastic, yet I'm still thinking about the sassy blonde from the party.

As hot as Sara and her girlfriend are, my cock gets even harder when I imagine Eden on her knees taking me.

As fucked up as it sounds, I have a feeling it's going to be her I get off to tonight . . .

KASH

TIRED AND HALF ASLEEP, I lean against the side of the ware-house, smoking a cigarette while I wait for Abe and Calvin to arrive.

They were both ordered to be here at seven A.M. sharp, yet it's already half past the hour.

My ass spends late nights dancing at the club, working my dick off. If I'm going to wake up at the ass crack of dawn to train these boys, then they better damn well be here on time and make it worth it to me.

This is the third time this week, they've been late.

Pissed off, I pull out my phone and toss my cigarette at the ground, about ready to give them both hell. Just as I get ready to scroll to Calvin's name, I hear a car coming down the gravel driveway, forcing me to put my phone back into my hoodie and look up.

I stand here with narrowed eyes, watching as the red Mazda comes to a stop next to my truck.

Abe is the first one to stumble out of the car, looking half-dead and hungover as shit.

Not to mention, his clothes are wrinkled and smell like whiskey as if he just crawled out of bed, in the same clothes he passed out in.

Should've damn well known.

"About fucking time, dicks. I told you to be here at seven. I was two seconds away from going back home and actually getting some damn sleep. You're wasting my time."

Abe falls against the side of the car and pulls his hat down over his eyes to shield them from the light. "Shit. We didn't get in until four. Cut us some slack, Kash. Honestly, I think I'm still drunk. This sucks dick."

I narrow my eyes at Calvin as he smiles cockily and jumps up on the hood of the car as if it's no big deal that I woke my ass up early this morning and wasted my damn time, waiting on them. "We're only thirty-five minutes late. You didn't waste that much time waiting on us. It took me over an hour to get Abe's ass up. I almost came alone, but figured you'd be more pissed than if we showed up late. We're here so can we just do this?"

"Nope." I lock up the warehouse and begin walking to my truck. I'm in no mood for this shit this morning. My exhausted ass has been here since six, getting a workout in. Time and dedication is exactly what I expect from them as well. "Next time you fuckers better be on time. I'm getting some damn sleep before my fight tonight. Get Abe home so he can sleep that shit off."

"Oh, come on!" Calvin screams in frustration. "We won't be late again. Don't do this shit. We both want this job and you know it. Abe was just being a dick this morning. It won't happen again."

"That's what you said two days ago. If you can't take this shit seriously, then neither can I. When I open my gym, I need one hundred fucking percent from the both of you." I jump into my truck and slam the door shut, before sticking my head out the window to look at them.

They both look like hell, tired and out of it. They're not ready for what I had in store for them this morning.

"See you guys back here later for the fights still or should I call Don and tell him to replace Abe?"

"Yeah," Calvin groans. "We'll be here. Abe's fight is two ahead of yours. He'll be good by then. He's not backing out."

"Good. Go get some damn sleep."

Abe gives me a thumbs up and almost falls over, before crawling back into the car.

These boys might think I'm being hard on them, but I don't expect my clients to wait. If they want to be trainers at my gym once it opens, then they need to show me dedication and hard work.

I'm not getting these dicks ready to be trainers just for them to not be reliable and me have to find new guys after just a few months.

I want long term and familiarity. A family.

They better shape up and fast.

Once I get back to the house, I walk inside to see Colt in the kitchen, cooking tacos in only his boxer briefs and a black beanie.

"What the hell are you doing up this early?" I toss my keys down on the table and sit down to pull my shoes off. "And why the hell are you cooking tacos for breakfast?"

"I'm drunk, high and hungry as shit. I'm going right back to bed after this. I feel like I'm going to die if I don't eat though."

"Whatever," I say with a laugh. "Just don't burn the damn house down while I'm sleeping. I'd hate to have to kill you."

I lay back on the couch and close my eyes, slowly dozing back off, until a hand runs over my chest and abs, before lowering and landing on my dick.

Grunting, I reach out and grip Harper's hand, stopping her from stroking my cock through my sweats.

"Leave him alone," Colt says from the kitchen with an amused laugh. "He's grumpy as hell this morning, babe."

"Oh, come on . . ." She smiles down at me and moans when I open my eyes to look at her. "But he looks so damn *tempting* just lying there in that mysterious hoodie of his. I want to strip it off with my teeth and run my hands all over what's beneath it."

Ignoring Colt, Harper leans in attempting to kiss me and work me up, but I bite her bottom lip, causing her to jump away from me with a squeal.

Her lips might work on other men, but not me.

"I don't do kisses," I growl out. "And I'm not in the mood to join in on your games. It's too early for this shit and I have a long night ahead of me."

"What did I tell you, babe?" Colt joins us in the living room, tossing a bottle of water to me, before grabbing up his girl and tossing her over his shoulder. "We don't need him to have fun. I have plenty of fun tricks up my sleeve. Let's eat first though."

Letting out an annoyed breath, I sit up and open the water, emptying the whole bottle in one drink, before tossing the empty plastic across the room, hitting Colt in the back of the head as he walks through the kitchen.

He just ignores me and slips his hand into Harper's panties, not caring that her pussy is on display for me.

Seriously? These two are crazy.

Tiredly, I make my way through the house, slamming my bedroom door shut and locking it behind me.

If I don't, then I know Harper will end up half-naked in my bed again, groping me until I give in and join them.

It's been happening more frequently lately and surprisingly

Colt is so chill and high most of the time he just goes with the flow.

Hell, sometimes he just sits back and smokes a blunt, watching all the ways I can make his girl moan out and beg.

Apparently, my body was built for pleasure since everyone seems to be using it lately.

There's only one person who seems to want nothing to do with it and for some reason I'm lying here, thinking about her once again . . .

chapter THREE

Eden

BY THE TIME KNIGHT SHOWS up at my door and lets himself in, as if he owns the damn place, I'm already running twenty minutes behind schedule.

It's infuriating.

He knew damn well ahead of time that I was starting back at the massage parlor this morning now that my father is back to take over his crew, yet he decided to take his precious time getting here as if it was the least important thing on his schedule today.

It doesn't surprise me one bit.

"You told me you were on the way over an hour ago. What the hell, Knight. This is not acceptable. Be here on time or see your son when I get *off* work. I can't be late again because of you."

He flashes me a cocky grin and leans against the door, crossing his huge arms. "Oh, calm down, Eden. If you lose your job at the parlor, you know damn well that daddy dearest will give you a job on one of his crews. Now, where's my son? I want to at least see him for a few minutes before you kick me out."

I let out a frustrated breath and point down the hall, fighting with everything in me not to lose my cool and scream at him. "He's in his room grabbing his backpack to go to the babysitter's. You have five minutes to say hi and don't you ever give me that shit again about me working for my father because *you* couldn't be here on time. If I wanted to work with my father, I would've chose to do so years ago. So be on time for now on because I won't wait next time."

"Damn, baby. Chill. You know I have a fight tonight. I was training late last night and had a hard time getting up. Now is the only time I can visit him today. Why the fuck are you always so uptight?"

"Because of you," I whisper yell, while pointing at his firm chest. "And watch your mouth. Alec can hear you. You don't think your deep voice carries in this house? You will show respect when you're in *my* home or you won't step foot inside again."

"Daddy! Daddy!" We both look over just in time to see Alec rush down the hall and jump into Knight's arms. "I didn't think you were coming to see me. Mommy said we were about to leave."

"Of course, I was coming to see you, bud." Knight bends down to set Alec back down to his feet, before giving him a frowny face and messing up his blonde hair. "But we have to make it fast because your mommy is rushing us. Says we only have a minute. You know how she gets."

Ugh. You son of a bitch.

He always finds some way to put the blame on me. Never fails, but I refuse to have this discussion in front of my son.

"But I want to spend time with you, daddy" Alec whines, while tugging on Knight's jacket. "Can't I just stay with you today? I'll be good. I promise. I have games and stuff in my bag."

Knight shakes his head and reaches out to grab Alec's chin to look him in the eyes. "Sorry, buddy. Not today. Daddy's busy."

I can practically see Alec's five-year old little heart shatter into a thousand pieces when he grabs the straps of his backpack and looks down at the ground, defeated.

"Busy," I mutter. "Just like every other time your son asks to spend the day with you. You need to get your priorities straight. You only see him once a week for twenty minutes if he's lucky."

My heart aches as I walk over and wrap my arms around Alec to comfort him. I hate seeing the disappointment on his face over and over again, each week. It never stops when it comes to his shitty father and it only makes me loath Knight more. "It's okay, sweetie. Hannah is excited for you to come see her today. I promise you'll have lots of fun with her. You always do."

"I know, mommy," Alec mutters against my stomach, while wiping at his wet eyes. "I guess. But I never get to see daddy. It's no fair. I want to see him."

"I know, baby." I kiss the top of his head, before rubbing it and forcing a smile. "Why don't you give your daddy a hug and then go put your bag in the jeep. I'll be out in a second. Okay, baby boy."

Without a word, Alec walks over and wraps his arms around Knight, holding onto him as if he never wants to let go. "Bye, daddy. I miss you today."

"Bye, little guy." He rubs the top of Alec's head, before brushing his thumb under his eye to wipe his tear away. "Daddy loves you and will see you soon. Don't cry. You're a big boy now."

"Okay. Love you too, daddy," he whispers, before walking away.

I wait until Alec is outside, before I lose it on Knight.

"The way you treat your son is bullshit!" I slam my keys

down onto the counter and run my hands down my face in frustration. "You can treat me like shit all you want. You have for the last seven years, but you will not do the same to *my* son. He depends on you. Be a fucking father for once. Put him before everything else, like a real man should. Show him you love him." I stop and release a long breath, my chest aching. "Dammit, Knight. You're breaking him down, little by little and soon he's going to stop trusting people. He barely lets people in as it is. He needs you and you know it. Show him you need him too."

"Shut the fuck up, Eden," he growls out, before punching the wall. "I don't have to listen to this shit anymore. Your fucking mouth is only a reminder of why I was never happy with you. You wanna know why I cheated over and over again? Why I never came home after a fight? Well, listen to your mouth and there's your answer."

"Oh yeah," I yell out. "How's my mouth for you now? Get. The. Fuck. Out." I point at the door with a shaky hand, fighting like hell not to burst into tears of hate and anger. "Leave the child support money and go. Now."

My whole body is shaking in anger at this point. I've never met someone in my entire life that can piss me off as much as Knight can. I wouldn't even care about the child support money if it hasn't been over six months since he's paid any.

"I'll have it for you in two weeks when I win my big fight. If you want it . . ." He steps into my breathing space and gives me a hard look as if to intimidate me. It has me taking a step back and sucking in a breath as his strong hands grip my waist when he speaks. "Then you can fucking come get it. I'm not being a little bitch and bringing it to you."

With that, he walks out the door and jumps into his car, making a huge scene as he pulls out of the driveway.

My heart is racing as I stand here and grip the counter. I will not fucking cry anymore. Not even out of anger will I allow that piece of shit to have my tears.

I take a few seconds to calm down and get myself back together, before I join Alec in the jeep.

He's sitting in the back, playing on his Nintendo 3DS as if he's already gotten over his father letting him down for the hundredth time this week.

I don't know how Knight does it. I feel guilty every single time I leave my son when it's for my own pleasure. Which is exactly why last night was so uncomfortable for me.

If it wasn't for Joni begging me to come, until I said yes, then I would've never went to some party to ogle over some male entertainers. That's just not what's important in my life right now. My son has top priority and always will.

I thought spending the whole night texting Hannah to check in on Alec would make me feel less guilty about leaving him, but it didn't.

All it took was a few seconds of enjoyment as one of the strippers practically fucked me against a wall, to make me lose my shit and run out of there, feeling like shit.

Made me feel like Knight.

That's the last thing I'll do to my son.

"Ready, mommy? Hannah is waiting for me. I want to show her my new game." He starts bouncing around, making all kinds of sound effects for his game. "I did it! I did it! I beat him."

I nod my head and smile at him through the rearview mirror. "Good job, baby. Let's go before mommy is really late."

I wish like hell I could be as strong as that kid. I try like heck to protect him, but sometimes I wish there was someone who could protect me and make me believe that everything in the world is going to be A-Okay.

Someone who could make us both believe, but I have my

doubts of that ever happening.

Especially with Knight in my life.

As soon as we pull up in front of Hannah's house, Alec jumps out, dragging his backpack behind him in excitement.

Hannah is already sitting outside on the front porch, waiting on him like she said she'd be.

She flashes us both a huge smile and bends down to talk to Alec once he reaches the top step. "I've got a great day planned for us, kid. But you have to let me beat you in your new game first. Deal?"

Alec smiles and shakes his head. "I can't do that! I'm really good! I don't think I can lose."

I stand back and watch as Alec begins looking around as if he's searching for someone.

"Is he here? Is he here?"

Hannah laughs and stands up. "Not today, buddy. It's not Monday."

"It isn't?" He tilts his head. "What day is it?"

"Saturday. You'll see him the next time you're here. I promise. Now give your mommy hugs and kisses so she can go to work and we can play this new game of yours." She pats his butt. "Hurry! Hurry!"

Laughing, Alec runs at me, throwing his little arms around my neck, squeezing. "Love you, mommy! I gotta go!"

I kiss his nose and smile. "Love you too, baby. Be good for Hannah, you hear me?"

He nods his head. "Yup! I'm always good. Promise. Come on, Hannah!"

"Who's he talking about?" I question with a smile once Alec runs through the front door in excitement. "He has a friend that comes over?"

"No, just my older brother Hunter I told you about,"

Hannah says with a smile. "He still brings Alec pancakes every Monday morning. They've become fast friends, which surprises me since it took so long for him to warm up to me. That's my brother though. Everyone loves him. They have fun together."

"That's nice of your brother to bring him pancakes still after all this time. They *are* his favorite." I find myself smiling at the idea that her brother is nice enough to do something like that. But I also find myself a little sad at the knowledge that this guy does something Knight isn't even capable of doing for his own child.

The last thing I want is for him to get attached to another man in his life that someday won't be there anymore.

"But don't worry. He never stays longer than an hour each week. It's usually just me here. He's a pretty busy guy."

"I trust you, Hannah. You take good care of him and he cares about you. I'm not worried."

"Hannah! Hurry! Come on!"

"I gotta go," she holds the door open and winks. "The kid's calling and I've got to make sure I beat him. Losing is getting pretty embarrassing."

"Good luck. He's already beat me ten times this week, even though I'm not even sure we're actually playing against each other." I laugh and pull out my phone, my stomach dropping when I see it's my work calling. "Shit, I've gotta run. Thank you!"

I cuss under my breath all the way to my jeep as I jump inside and quickly answer my phone, out of breath.

"I'm on my way. I'm so sorry. I had to wait for that asshole son of a bitch. He showed up right when I was about to leave . . ."

"You're fine," Riley says with a laugh. "Just wanted to make sure you'll be here in time for your first appointment. I have you booked at eight. If not I was going to call them and try to set it back a bit for you."

"Yes," I say quickly. "I'll be there in twelve minutes. Thank you so much. I owe you. I promise I'll make up for it."

Relief washes over me as I hang up the phone and take a few seconds to calm down and catch my breath.

If it weren't for Riley being my boss, I don't know what I'd do. She's been lenient on me far too many times in the past, but taking advantage of her kindness is the last thing I want to do.

And Knight keeps pushing me to do that, making me feel like total crap.

So I'll do everything in my power to prove to her over and over again just how much I appreciate this job.

Showing appreciation is very important to me. It's something Knight has never shown me over the years, yet I was stupid enough to let him in anyway. It only makes it more important that I show it to others.

I promise to be better than him in every possible way I can. Especially when it comes to my son.

And when I'm ready to let another man in mine and Alec's lives, you better believe, I'll make sure he's better than Knight in every way too . . .

chapter FOUR

KASH

AFTER SPITTING BLOOD, I SWING out, hitting Zack with a right hook, shaking him up and causing him to stumble back.

I stand still as he circles around me, looking for his opportunity to strike. I'm giving him one chance and then I'm taking his ass out. This has gone on for too long.

These people came for a show and that's what I give them, even if it means me taking it easy in the beginning, giving my opponent a chance to get a few hits in.

Fighting to catch his breath, Zack swipes his left foot out, but I lift my leg up right as he tries kicking it out from under me. This must give him a reason to try harder, because before I know it he swings out with his elbow and connects it to my right cheekbone before following up with a right hook.

I falter back a few steps, but I'm able to catch myself and connect my right fist to his jaw, sending him back against the ropes.

Blood splatters across his face, causing him to spit red onto his chest, before he comes at me, knocking me against the ropes.

He punches me in the ribs a few times, cornering me in, before I plow my knee into his gut and swing out with my elbow, hitting him in this nose.

He's worn out now, completely out of stamina and I know what I have to do. There's no way he's going to give up before it's over, no matter how exhausted he is.

I need to put him down.

Standing straight, I flex my shoulders and wipe the blood from my lip, before swinging out one last time, my fist connecting hard with Zack's already swollen jaw.

Cheers of excitement fill the warehouse as he drops to the mat, knocked out cold.

Adrenaline courses through me as I throw my arms up and look around at all the people here to see me tonight. This warehouse isn't the biggest, but it's cram packed and I've come to recognize some of the faces over the months.

As much as I enjoy it though, I don't allow myself to get swallowed up by it and let it consume me like some fighters do. Fighting isn't really what I *want* to do.

Training and helping others is my main goal.

I don't even give myself a few seconds to catch my breath, before I make my way over to Zack to check on him.

One of his guys is standing over him and squirting water over his face to help him wake up, so I give him a few minutes to gather himself before reaching down and helping him up to his feet.

"Good fight, man," I throw one of my arms around him as I hold him up and encourage him to keep fighting. I've known this kid for years and the feeling sucks knowing that I probably broke his nose during this fight. "You've got a lot of heart and that's exactly why you deserve to be in that ring. Got it?"

He nods his head, showing appreciation as I check on his nose. It's definitely broken. "Appreciate it, man." He stops a second to catch his breath, before speaking again. "There was a slim chance in hell I'd beat you tonight, but I wasn't going down without a fight. Your father taught me well and once you take over this place and get all set up, I'm hoping you'll train me too."

"Of course, man." Mention of my father has me fighting back my emotions. It's moments like this that made me stop fighting after he passed just after my twentieth birthday.

It's been three years now, but I still struggle with his absence. He was a huge part of my life and every little reminder that he's no longer here kills me.

But it's time for me to man up.

Every win brings me closer to the money necessary to get my training gym up and running. It's been a dream of mine ever since I was a kid and I used to watch my dad train his men.

I always thought we'd open a gym together in the future, but that dream was crushed when he got sick and passed away.

I took a break from fighting shortly after that and just picked it back up in hopes of finally living that dream and making him proud.

Stripping became my biggest income toward making that happen a while back, but these fights are only going to make the process move faster. It's the *only* reason I'm fighting.

Not for the afterparties where everyone gets shitfaced or the pleasure of dominating someone in the ring. For the money.

By the end of my second fight, I'm completely drenched in sweat and every inch of my body aches with every single move I make.

Not only from the fights, but from the training and dancing I've been doing this whole week, leading up to tonight.

And these fights, are nothing compared to the fight I'll be

training to take on in a couple of weeks. It's going to take a lot more preparation and dedication than what I've been doing for the last six months since I've come back.

Fighting in the warehouse is just a warm up to the big guys, I've been working my ass off to fight.

That's where the real prize money sits.

"Good fights, man." Abe appears next to me, his face swollen and bruised from his fight earlier. I can tell with one look in his eyes that he's ashamed he messed up his chance of winning tonight. "These other guys didn't stand a chance against you. Even they knew it. Congrats."

I smile and nod my head, before patting his back. "You'll get your win next time, man. Just let my ass know if you want to set up more training sessions. I'll make time for you, but you've gotta show me you want it. Got it?"

He nods and forces a smile. "I might need that. I need to get back on track. No more late night partying for my dumb ass. Especially before a fight night."

"Alright, man." I throw the strap of my bag over my shoulder, ready to get out of here before I can get stopped again. "I have an appointment to set up. I'll see you Monday morning for training."

I'm just on my way out the door, when Callie rushes over and throws her arms around me, stopping me from walking.

"Congratulations on your wins tonight! Watching you fight is even better than watching you dance. I'm impressed, Kash."

Callie's been at Walk of Shame more than enough times for me to recognize her by face now. Not to mention, she's been spending a lot of money on private dances from me over the last two weeks.

Her coming here tonight was just her way of trying to get me alone without the craziness of the hundreds of women at the club. More of a chance for her to get what she wants.

Which is me, naked, and on top of her.

"Thanks, Callie." I offer her a smile, while taking my shirt and running it over my sweaty chest, watching as she practically salivates at the sight of my hard body. "Appreciate you coming."

Not wanting to deal with her groping me and trying to work her way into my bed, I begin walking again in hopes she'll take off with her friends and forget about me.

"Kash! Wait . . ."

Releasing a slow breath, I stop and turn around to face her, looking her over in her tight jeans and her very sexy V neck top with a laced-up front. Her huge breasts are spilling out everywhere. Cleary, she's dressed to get attention tonight.

As tempting as she may look, I'm not looking for meaningless fun tonight. I've had enough *fun* over the years and it's time to take shit more seriously. I'm a different man than I was when I first started dancing at *Walk of Shame*. I'm slowly beginning to see that.

"Me and my friends are going to the after party. Will I see you there?" Her eyes scan me over from head to toe, taking in my sweaty body, as she waits for my answer.

Unfortunately, she's not going to get the one she's looking for tonight.

I shake my head. "Not tonight. You ladies have fun without me."

Disappointment washes over her eager face as her girls walk over to join her. "You sure? It'll be fun. I'll make sure of it."

"Yeah," one of her friends joins in. "We're a pretty fun group. We'll keep you entertained. Maybe you can invite a few of your friends, too."

I let out a small laugh, feeling a bit teamed up on now. Double teaming might've worked in the past for me, but not now. "Sorry, ladies. I have somewhere to be. Not gonna happen."

Before they can attempt to entice me anymore, I rush

outside and jump into my lifted truck, checking the time.

"Shit."

Pulling out of the parking lot, I dial Riley's number in hopes she's still at work.

I'm surprised when she answers it before the second ring.

"Did you win?" she asks immediately. "I've been staring at this darn phone waiting to hear news. Spill it."

I smile into the phone. "Hi to you too, Riley."

"Oh, please. I've known you long enough that I shouldn't have to say hello anymore. Now, answer my question, Kash."

"Yes." I pull out into traffic and head toward *Sensual Touches*, hoping like hell she says yes to what I'm about to ask. "Think you can fit me in tonight for a quick rub down with one of your massage therapists? I feel like I've been hit by a damn semi."

"Better hurry up. I'm only saying yes since you won tonight and I think you deserve it." I hear her laugh into the phone before she continues. "One of my ladies is looking for some extra cash. I'm sure she won't mind staying back for a bit and fitting you in for the night."

"Thank you, babe. Be there in five."

Hanging up, I speed up, taking the side roads in hopes there won't be any traffic to slow me down.

The place closes in less than twenty-five minutes and I'm in desperate need of this relaxation *tonight*. I don't care if it takes me dropping to my knees and begging this woman Riley mentioned.

I barely park my truck, before I'm jumping out and rushing for the door as if my damn life depends on it.

The woman leaving the parlor spins around to check me out as I hold the door open for her to pass me.

"Maybe I need to get a job here," she says with a smile of admiration. "Thanks."

"For what?" I question with a small laugh.

"Just for being so handsome." Her face turns red as she waves and turns around to leave. "Damn, I wish I was single."

Riley is standing right inside the door, grinning from ear to ear when I walk inside. "Couldn't wear a shirt, huh? As if you don't distract my clients enough already."

"You don't want me wearing that sweaty ass thing in here. Trust me." I lean against the counter and wait for Riley to tell me which room. "I pretty much used it as a towel after my fight and tossed it in the truck."

"And you're telling me some girl didn't steal it to take home and sleep in it? Surprising . . ." Riley looks away from the computer and smiles down at her phone when it rings. "Room four. Hurry up. Eden's just grabbing some supplies from the back so do her a favor and be ready."

"Eden?" My heart skips a beat at the mention of her name. It's not a very common one.

"Hey, handsome. Hang on a sec," she says into the phone, before answering me. "Yeah. She's one of my girls that's been away for a bit. You haven't met her yet. She's good though. I promise."

A huge ass smile takes over my face as I picture the Eden I met the other night. "Sassy blonde?"

"Yeah, that's her." She looks surprised. "How'd you know? Did you come in when I was gone one day?"

I begin backing up, even more eager for this massage now. "Later, Riley. Tell Cale about my fights since I don't have time."

I ignore her question and hurry down the hall, wanting to get to Eden's room, before she does.

Hopefully this will give me a chance to get to know the woman behind the sass . . .

chapter FIVE

Eden

IT'S ALMOST CLOSING TIME AND I'm completely exhausted and emotionally drained at this point, just ready to call it a night so I can curl into bed with my son and spend time with him.

I can tell by the tone of his voice that he's missing me and it makes my heart ache that I can't be there for him. He doesn't deserve to have to miss two parents at the same time. He should *always* have one of us there.

"Mommy will be there soon, Alec. I promise. Can you be good for Hannah for just a bit longer? It won't be long. I promise."

"Yes, mommy. I can do that. I be good for Hannah," he says with a yawn. "Love you, mommy. Byyye."

"Love you, too, baby. Thank you."

I can hear Hannah in the background asking for the phone back, before she reassures me it's fine if I'm a little late tonight.

As much as I hate being away from Alec longer than I have to–I need the money.

Knight isn't doing his part and there's no way I'm relying on anyone else to take care of my family for me. That's not who I am or who I ever want to be, no matter how hard my father tries pushing money on me.

It's up to *me* to give him the life he deserves, even if that means me taking on extra shifts once or twice a week or staying later here and there. I'll do whatever it takes.

Shoving my phone into my small apron, I grab for some more oil, lotion and a few candles, before heading back to my room to stock up.

According to Riley, my last client of the night should already be here by now and most likely set up in my room and ready for me to start.

I'm counting on that so I can get the job done and out of here as quickly as possible.

Stopping in front of the door, I knock and wait for whoever is on the other side to let me know it's okay to come in.

"I'm decent." A deep voice calls out.

A lot of the guys that come here take this as an opportunity to show me the *goods,* by tricking me to believe they're ready, but they're standing in my room completely naked on display for me to see.

I've grown to expect it at this point, but today has been exceptionally bad. My eyes can only handle so much in one damn day.

Please be covered up. Please no more dong and balls tonight . . .

Upon stepping into my room, relief washes over me as my eyes immediately land on a firm body, covering the massage table.

The client is facing down, the bottom half of his body covered by a sheet, only giving me a view of his muscular back, arms and legs.

"Well, congratulations. You're my first honest client to-night. I'm slightly impressed." I smile as the guy laughs into the pillow. "So, thank you for not showing me your balls. I've seen more than my fair share tonight."

"Most women don't thank me for that, but you're welcome, I think." His back muscles flex as he adjusts himself to get more comfortable. "You did me a huge favor by fitting me in at last min-ute tonight. The least I can do is not show you my balls . . . unless you ask of course. Then I guess I would owe you."

His sense of humor has me laughing as I wash my hands and dry them off. Maybe sticking around to fit this guy in will be entertaining at least. That usually helps the time to pass. Plus, I could use a laugh after such a stressful day.

"I appreciate that, but I'm one hundred and ten percent pos-itive I won't be asking to see them . . ." I pause, searching for a name as I empty the lotion and candles from my apron. "What should I call you? Bob? George? Kenneth?"

"Kash," he says, sounding amused. "Those names are fuck-ing horrible, by the way. I hope like hell I don't look as bad as those names sound."

"I hope not too," I joke. "I'd have to charge extra then."

"And fuck. I'd pay it too," he says with a laugh.

Once I get closer to the bed, I find myself swallowing as I look his body over, taking in the perfection, while I blindly reach for my oil and open the new bottle.

He definitely doesn't look as bad as those names sound.

Being this close really displays how beautiful and sculpted this man's body is. A woman's eyes can definitely appreciate the sight I have in front of me right now.

Just hopefully my hands don't appreciate it *too* much.

I can honestly say over touching has never been an issue with any of my clients, but this body is definitely a dirty temptation.

Take a deep breath and relax . . . deep breath and relax.

The music is already playing and Kash looks to be completely comfortable and ready for me to start, so I take another deep breath, like I've couched myself and say my usual lines.

"My name is Eden, by the way." I walk around to the top of the bed and squirt some oil into my hands, preparing to rub them down his muscular body. "I'm going to start at your shoulders and work my way down. Let me know if there's a certain spot you'd like me to focus on."

He lets out a sexy little growl, the moment my hands rub the first tense spot, digging in deep. I might've let out a little growl myself, feeling his firm body under my touch, but I'm hoping he didn't notice.

"I'll take whatever you can give me within the next thirty minutes," he says, his voice deep and sexy. "Honestly, I would've been down for begging you at this point and I don't beg very often. Fuuuck me, keep going, Eden. I like it hard and rough. Don't fucking take it easy on me."

The way he says *fuck* has my heart beating fast in my chest, feeling a bit excited. I didn't know that word could sound so sexy coming out of someone's mouth, until now.

"Is that you begging?" I tease.

"You'd know if I was begging, Eden," he growls out, his hard muscles flexing beneath my hands. "It'd be pleasurable for the both of us and there's no doubt I'd get what I want in the end. Trust me . . . I'm as honest as they come and it would most definitely end with you coming . . ."

If my heart wasn't beating out of my chest before, it is now. I've never had a man on my table before that had the power to make me as hot and bothered as I am at this very moment.

His words have me sweating, but there's no way I'm giving him the pleasure of letting him know he's getting to me.

Without speaking, I begin working my way further down his back side, being careful not to focus my eyes on his firm ass for too long.

I feel like such a pervert right now, but there's no denying his body feels fantastic beneath my fingertips and I like it.

It's when I work my way back up his thick legs that he speaks again, really making me think dirty. "You don't have to be careful not to get my ass, Eden. My whole back side needs attention." Before I can say anything, he reaches behind him and yanks the sheet off, revealing his muscular ass to me. "Work it nice and good."

"Really?!" I pull my hands from his legs and squirt more oil in my palm. "Out of all the places I can focus on, you choose your ass?"

"Have you ever had an ass massage, Eden?"

"No," I admit, while rubbing my hands together. "I've never really had much of any kind of a massage, to be honest."

"Then, you have no idea what you're missing out on." He places his hands on the side of the table and pushes up when he speaks. "Maybe we should switch places. Every woman deserves to be rubbed and taken care of by a man."

"As tempting as that sounds, I'm going to have to pass." I shake my head, fighting my smile. "Now lay back down so I can do my job. Time is almost up."

Thinking he's going to listen, I get ready to get back to work, but before my hands can touch his glorious ass, he's hopping off the table, and picking me up to take his place.

My breath gets sucked right out of me as he sets me on the edge of the table, his naked body pressing between my legs.

"Oh my God! What are you doing?" I try my best not to look at his naked body, as he backs away from me and throws a fresh sheet over the pillow, but I can't help but to peek between my fingers.

Just a quick glimpse of his dick is enough to let me know this guy is packing where it counts.

Oh holy hell . . .

"Giving you a massage," he says casually, as if this is somehow normal, when this is anything but. "Don't worry you can keep your clothes on." Grabbing my waist with force, he flips me over and pushes my head down into the pillow, causing me to move my hands from my face.

Has me thinking dirty things–like how he might handle a woman in bed. I bet he's rough and very thorough, making sure to hit every spot.

Dammit, Eden. Don't go there . . .

"You do realize it's *my* job to massage you, right?" I try to ask calmly. "I work here. This is weird and could possibly get me fired."

"It won't get you fired and this is not weird," he says with a hint of laughter. "I never find a man taking care of a woman to be weird. Now lay down and relax because I'm not leaving without giving you a taste."

I suck in a breath and close my eyes to the feel of his strong hands on my shoulders, taking charge. "Can you at least put a towel on so you're not massaging me naked? Now that *is* weird."

"If that's what you really want."

"I do," I answer quickly, even though I can barely even convince myself I'm telling the truth.

I feel his warm breath hit my ear, before he speaks against it, causing chills to run over my flesh. "Are you sure? I massage better in the *nude*. It's a proven fact."

A moan escapes me as his strong hands work down my back to grab the bottom of my shirt, lifting it up over my bra. As soon as his big hands meet my bare skin, I feel my body heat up from his touch and instantly melt into him.

I barely even notice him undo my bra and at this point, I don't care, because his hands feel fantastic.

"Yes," I groan as he begins to rub harder, going deeper, almost distracting me from the fact that he still hasn't put a towel on. "Please put a towel on. This is already unusual for me. It's not every day I allow a client to put their hands on me. Just please . . ."

His hands leave me for a few seconds, my body immediately missing the feel of his hands touching me and taking care of me. I've definitely been missing out over the years, always being on the giving end and not the receiving end.

Holy shit . . . this man's hands are pure magic.

My body melts again, the second his hands return and I find myself relaxing and just letting him take charge as he lifts my shirt higher and moves his way up my body, touching me so damn good.

I'm so used to overseeing everything, that it feels fantastic just letting go for a few moments and leaving things in the hands of someone else.

Even if it is a half-naked stranger with a body like a Greek God.

As soon as his hands find their way down to my thighs to spread them, I suck in a breath and grip the bottom of the table.

"Relax, Eden." He lets out a deep laugh and lifts my leg higher, sliding his hands up my shorts a little, causing my body to react from his closeness.

It feels so sexual, but so damn relaxing at the same time. I'm not sure if I should be turned on from this, but I totally am. No wonder why these men show up naked and pop boners from my hands rubbing them.

This is a lot more erotic than I ever knew. Truthfully, I tried to block any ideas of my job being sexy in any way. Was the only way to handle it.

But thanks to Kash . . .

"I'm not going to massage your pussy. *That* kind of massage, I make sure I'm naked for and you've already forced me to cover up. So, you're out of luck."

There he goes again being sexy and humorous at the same damn time. The perfect balance.

"Don't talk." I moan out and bite my lip as he switches to my right thigh now, getting extremely close to my vagina, but being respectful enough to keep a safe distance. His grip on my thigh is tight. Honestly, this feels too good to make him stop, so I'm going to just go with the flow for once. "Just rub . . . yes . . . right there. Oh wow . . ."

It's completely quiet for a few minutes, him taking the time to take care of me, before he speaks again, his voice sounding a bit breathy.

"We're going to have to set up a time for me to give you a *real* massage, Eden. You're too fucking tense and ten minutes isn't even close to enough time for me to take care of you the right way. Your body needs dedication."

Releasing my thigh, he moves his way up my body to clasp my bra and pull my shirt back down.

The way his fingertips graze my flesh on the way down, causes goosebumps to cover my body and heat me up at the same time.

"Yeah well, I don't have a lot of time to take care of myself these days. I'm not what's most important in my life. I haven't been for a while now."

"Then you should be that for someone else," he says as I flip over and sit up to see him facing the wall and pulling his sweats up. "Just another reason for you to let me make you important even if it's only for thirty minutes out of your day. It doesn't sound like other men have done that for you. They were fucking idiots and obviously didn't know how to take care of a woman."

I watch his back muscles flex as he reaches for the door handle and pauses. "Get my number from Riley. And by the way . . ." he turns around and faces me, showing his face for the first time tonight.

My mouth drops open, me immediately recognizing him from last night. "It was nice seeing you again, Eden."

My gaze wanders over his firm body, taking in every dip and muscle, before lowering down to his very noticeable erection.

It's so damn thick and well . . . on display for me. He doesn't even attempt to hide it.

Holy hell.

With a small smirk, he exits the room, leaving me to sit here in surprise with my hands over my face.

Kash is the stripper that almost completely made me come undone last night from his body. I should've known there was something familiar about this guy.

He had the ability to work me up just as he did last night, before I rushed out the door, needing to get away.

Who would've thought a male stripper could have a sweet and caring side to go with his filthy mouth?

I have a feeling that could be a very bad combination for me if I agree to taking his number.

But I have to admit that the opportunity is more than tempting and temptation is something I haven't felt in a long time.

And I've already felt it twice with Kash.

With my mind racing, I quickly clean up and head out front to clock out.

"Everything okay?" Riley asks with a small smile, while flipping off the lights.

I nod my head and grip the strap of my purse. "I'm fine." I lie. "Why?"

She stops to look me over with amusement. "Your entire body is flushed." She raises a brow as I walk with her to the door. "Your last appointment go well?"

"Went fine," I say quickly. A little too quickly. "Just anxious to get home."

"Good." Riley gives me a quick nod and heads for her new car. "See you later, babe. Let me know if there's *anything* you might need."

I wait until she jumps into her car, before I throw my hand over my face in embarrassment. By *anything*, she meant Kash's number. I know that without a doubt.

So much for pretending Kash didn't get to me tonight. Even my damn boss can see it . . .

KASH

AFTER I PULL UP BEHIND of *Walk of Shame*, I park my truck and jump out, before pulling the tailgate down and jumping onto it.

The cool night air feels good against my face, giving me a moment to relax and think for the first time in days.

Taking my time, I lay back and place my arms behind my head, getting lost in thought.

Between working the club, training for my upcoming fights and helping my guys out, I haven't had a moment to breathe and actually enjoy it in who knows how long.

My shift begins in ten minutes, so you better fucking believe, I'm taking every second I can get, before I have to go in there and get groped by a ton of crazy women that will most likely try to take me home tonight.

Closing my eyes, I take in a deep breath, before slowly releasing it and reaching into my hoodie for a cigarette.

As the smoke fills my lungs, I allow myself a few moments

to think about Eden for the first time in the three days since I've seen her.

It's not that I haven't wanted to think about her, because trust me, I've wanted to. But every time my thoughts stray her way, I get distracted by someone interrupting me or my ass is just too exhausted to make sense of anything that happened that night at *Sensual Touches*.

After her running out on me at her friend's party last week, I wanted to take advantage of the time I had her stuck in a room with me, even if it was only for thirty minutes.

I wanted a chance for her to see me as something other than just a male fucking stripper that knows how to make a whole room of women *hot* and *wet*.

I'm so much more than that.

I'm a man that shows dedication to my woman and fights with everything in me to keep her feeling safe and cared for in every single way.

I hated hearing that Eden hasn't experienced that kind of dedication from a man before. If she had, then she would know what a damn massage feels like.

Only makes me want to take care of her more.

"What the hell . . ." I run my hand over my face and think about how it felt to have her soft body beneath my fingers.

As soon as I slid my hands up her little shorts, feeling the heat from between her legs, I got hard and I know without a doubt that she noticed on my way out. Her wide eyes as she looked me over, said it all.

But how the hell could I *not* get hard from touching her? She's so damn beautiful.

How could any man in his right mind not want to feel that day in and day out? I was completely exhausted and sore, but rubbing her and taking care of her overpowered any of that shit and made me forget about myself.

I would've spent the entire night on her body if that's what she allowed me to do. Hell, I even offered to take care of her another night, but I have a feeling I won't hear from her.

Most women would've called me as soon as they got off work, but Eden isn't like most women. I can already see that and it has me completely intrigued by her, wanting to know more.

I just hope I get that chance. I can tell there's something holding her back. I just need to find out what or *who*.

"You're late."

Taking one more drag off my cigarette, I toss it and sit up to see Stone looking down at me. He's completely covered in sweat, looking beat. A typical night here at the club for all of us, no matter how big or small the crowd is.

It takes a lot out of you physically and emotionally working at a place like this.

"It's slow in there. They'll manage without me for a few minutes." I hope.

"True. Sara can hold the shit down at the bar for a while. Just thought I'd let your ass know because you seemed lost in your own little world over here, hiding in that damn hideous hoodie of yours." He pulls out his phone and smiles as if he's the happiest man alive. "My future wife is telling me to hurry my ass home to her. Fuck, I love saying that. Not sure I'll ever get used to it."

It's been six months since Stone and Sage have made things official with them and just a few weeks ago, he got down on one knee and asked her to marry him.

"I still can't believe she agreed to marry your crazy ass." I tease, just to work him up. "She's so much hotter and smarter than you. Pretty much better in every damn way."

"What can I say?" He begins backing away in a hurry. "She

sees the best in me. I got lucky and hopefully one day some hot chick will find the best in you. But I doubt it." His mouth curves into a smirk.

Laughing, I jump down from my truck and grab for my gym bag. "I won't argue that. You got damn lucky. Tell the wifey I miss her."

"Fuck no. She's mine." He gives me the middle finger with both hands, before spinning around and waving his hand back at me. "See ya, asshole. The crazies are out tonight so have fun with that shit."

"See ya, dick." Still laughing, I shake my head and toss my bag over my shoulder, before making my way through the back entrance of the club.

The first thing my eyes land on is Kage standing outside of the locker room, keeping two drunk girls busy that keep trying to sneak past him. They're most likely trying to get to Myles who should've just gotten off stage a few minutes ago.

Stone wasn't wrong. Shit.

"Back up, ladies. You're not allowed back here." Kage shakes his head and gives me an amused look when he sees me leaning against the wall, watching him struggle. "Enjoying the show, dick head?"

I lift a brow and push away from the wall, drawing the girls' attention my way. "I always enjoy a good show. You know this, Kage."

"Me too. A hell of a lot. So have fun with these two. They haven't given up once tonight." With a smirk, he backs away from the girls, and watches as they come at me, pulling at my hoodie as if they want to see what's under it.

"Who's this hottie?" the blonde asks, while pushing my hood back and touching my facial hair. "Please tell me you're one of the strippers. We need this thing off. Like right now."

I feel her friend come up behind me, pressing her body against mine as she reaches around to grab my chest and grope me. "Nice and firm just how we like it. We definitely need this thing off." She runs her hands down my abs, stopping when I grab them before they get to where they're headed. "Rough and mysterious. I like it. Very hot."

The blonde must take this as a good opportunity to jump back in, because before I know it, she's grabbing my cock and running her hands over my jeans, while her friend has me distracted.

With a growl, I grab her hand and lean in to whisper in her ear. "Don't touch what you can't handle. I'm rough all around. Really fucking rough."

With that, the girls back away, looking me over with heated eyes, while giggling to each other. "We were about to head out for the night, but I think we've changed our minds. See you out there, hoodie."

I turn to Kage when he laughs. "Some kind of security you are, asshole." I shake my head and shove him away from the door, before disappearing into the locker room.

I'm not sure if I should be surprised that the back door didn't do shit to keep the women off me. I'm not even on the clock yet and my dick's already been groped.

Might as well start a count for the night.

Hell, the highest I got in one night was fifty-two times and I was only here for four hours. That shit still surprises me.

Myles is just stepping out of the shower, walking naked to get to his locker when I make my way over to mine.

"Those crazy chicks still out there?" He laughs in disbelief and pulls his jeans on, without even bothering to dry off. "They followed me back here over twenty minutes ago." He rubs a red spot on his chest. "Hell, I think one of them even bit me. That shit did not feel good."

I set my bag down and dig inside for some jeans and a black shirt. "They just walked away *after* groping my ass. Well, actually my damn dick, I should say. But I'll take that over being bitten. I only like that shit in the bedroom."

"Ha! Well, good luck getting rid of them now," he says with a lopsided grin. "They won't be going anywhere tonight. Especially if they've gotten a feel of your man meat."

"Yeah . . ." I slip my jeans on and button them. "Well, I'm not stripping tonight. I'm working the bar. It's all Colt for the next five hours. So, good luck to that motherfucker."

Myles laughs, while running his hand through his wet, dark hair. "I'll be sure to wish him luck on the way out the door. It might not be a packed house tonight, but apparently, it's a night for all the crazies to be here."

"So I heard . . . and witnessed."

This only makes me thankful I'm working the bar tonight and not the floor. I seriously don't think I could handle all that shit tonight.

Not that the bar is much better, but it's definitely less demanding and keeps your dick from being fondled every two seconds by strange women.

After I toss my bag into my locker, I make my way over to the bar, stopping when I see Cale trying to make his way through the crowd of women.

He can barely walk around this place without women swooning over him and begging him to go back to his stripper days.

I grip his shoulder. "Hey, man. I needed a few minutes to myself tonight before coming inside. Just wanted to let you know I'm late with clocking in."

Cale gives me the same understanding smile he's given me

since I first walked in that door almost two years ago. "You've been here long enough to know when it's okay to not be here right on time. I trust you boys. You haven't let me down yet. I'll let you know when you do."

"Thanks, man." I slap his back and quickly make my way behind the bar to clock in, before Sara can strangle me for leaving her hanging.

Sara immediately greets me with a sad smile, while looking my face over. She hasn't seen me since my fight the other night. "That pretty face is all bruised up and I hate it. I heard you kicked ass though. That's hot."

I shake my head and laugh. "My face will heal. This is nothing compared to what's to come in a couple of weeks. I might even be lucky if you recognize me after that one."

"I have faith you'll kick ass then, too." She winks and then walks away to help a few girls, giving me time to slip my hoodie back on and get comfortable.

After being here for two hours, I lean over the bar top to take a moment, while it's slow on drink orders and look over to see Colt is looking completely exhausted and worn down.

He's trying to work his body to *Anywhere* by 112, but from the looks of it, his ass can hardly even dance at this point.

So, I jump up onto the bar and decide to help his tired ass out and give him a quick break.

Slowly, I make my way across the bar top, grabbing at the bottom of my hoodie as I stop and grind my hips, drawing attention of the women my way.

Biting my bottom lip, I move the hoodie up slightly with each move I make, hoping to tease them and make them want more.

This must get their attention, because before I know it, there's a shit ton of women rushing over to throw their money my way.

Winding my fists up in the fabric, I thrust my hips, slowly and move the hoodie higher, until I'm pulling it over my head and tossing it aside.

Once I'm down to my shirt and jeans, I run my hands down my chest, moving them seductively down my body, stopping once I reach my cock.

I run my hand over it a few times, keeping my eyes closed as I thrust my hips and get lost in the music.

This has whoever's sitting in the stool in front of me, letting out a small gasp as if she's turned on by me touching myself.

Satisfied, I drop to my knees, flex my chest and pull my shirt over my head and toss it aside, before I grind my hips slowly, as if I'm fucking the person below me.

It's then that I look down to see *her* sitting on the stool, watching me with curiosity.

I have no idea when she got in the room, but I'm guessing it was right when I decided to draw all the attention my way.

I'm just glad that I have *her* attention along with the rest of the room since last time she saw me dance, she pretended not to enjoy it.

Well that was before she got the chance to get to know me. I don't see her looking away now and it has my body reacting.

Her green eyes land on mine and she looks nervous as if she's just been caught doing something she wasn't meant to, but she doesn't turn away.

Her eyes stay on me, taking me in as if she wishes it were her *hands* on me instead.

Well, damn. I definitely wasn't expecting to see her here, but I'll take this any day over just a phone call . . .

chapter SEVEN

Eden

MY HEART SPEEDS UP WITH excitement, my palms becoming sweatier with each move of Kash's insanely sexy body up on the bar.

I can barely handle looking at him right now, without remembering the glimpse I got of his naked body last week at *Sensual Touches*, when I lost my battle at *not* peeking between my fingers.

There's no denying the fact that he's absolutely beautiful and I've spent some time since then, pleasuring myself to that image, wondering what it would be like to experience the real thing.

Knight is the only man I've been with sexually and if I have to be honest, he never took the time to take care of me and make sure I felt good. It was always about him and what he needed.

He was a selfish man in more ways than one.

Kash on the other hand, gives off the impression that he's all about taking care of a woman and making her feel good in every way. He showed that by giving up his massage to give me one, instead. It's definitely a desirable quality in a man that seems to be extremely rare.

But as much as I enjoy looking at and fantasizing about Kash, and all the things he can do to me, I need to be careful when it comes to men and letting them in. My son still comes first over my needs and I made a promise to myself the day he was born that I would never be selfish and put him in a situation that might hurt him in the end.

The only reason I'm even here in the first place tonight is to give Kash back the hundred dollar tip he left me a few nights ago. I don't deserve it and after thinking it over for the last few days, I've come to the conclusion that I need to give it back.

It's the right thing to do and I'm not leaving here without him accepting it.

He was barely even in my room for thirty minutes and ten of those minutes were spent on him massaging *me*.

I can't accept the tip. I'd feel too guilty keeping it, even though I could use the extra money right now.

Plus, I have to admit there was a small part of me that wanted to see him again, no matter how hard I tried to convince myself otherwise.

There was something about the way Kash talked to me during our time together that had me completely intrigued, wanting to know more about him and what kind of guy he truly is.

Not just the male entertainer I got a glimpse of that first night. The real him.

I was hoping to maybe get a few minutes to do that tonight, but from the looks of things, I'm not so sure now.

When Riley told me he was bartending tonight, instead of dancing, I figured it'd be the best night to stop in and give him his money back, *without* having a crazy group of women surrounding him.

I was completely wrong. These women are going crazy over him and inside, I might be just a little bit too.

'Cause holy hell . . .

That night I met him at Joni's party doesn't do him any justice as to how he's moving his body right now on that bar. Sort of makes me wish I would've stayed longer to see him dance.

The way his strong hands move over his hard body as he grinds his hips with perfect rhythm is completely seductive and hypnotizing.

Seeming to ignore all the women around him, Kash leans over and grabs my hands, placing them on his hard chest as he continues moving his body in front of me.

The way he looks at me is almost enough to make me believe we're the only two people in the room.

How he can manage to do that, when the room is full of beautiful women, wanting to get to him, is beyond crazy.

Some of them are even practically climbing on top of me right now, wanting a taste of this man.

But I can't help but to let him draw me in anyway, getting lost in this moment with him as if no one else is around.

Sitting up straight, he slowly runs my hands lower, with each thrust of his hips, stopping before they can reach the very visible bulge in his pants.

My heart is beating out of my chest at this point, wondering what it would feel like to go lower. To just give in for two seconds and be selfish for once in my life.

I feel like such a pervert right now. Kash has a way of doing that to me.

Leaving my hands on his body, he moves in closer to wrap his hands into the back of my hair and hold me in place as if to tell me he's dancing for me and only me.

Keeping his eyes on me and only me, he jumps down from the bar and picks me up, wrapping my legs around his waist, before he buries his face into my neck as he dances.

The way he does it is so sensual and personal, giving off a whole new vibe than that first night when all it did was make me feel dirty.

I feel anything *but* right now.

His hands move from my hips down to cup my ass as his mouth brushes up my neck. Without even thinking about it, I lean my head back exposing myself for him.

He sucks and nips at my neck, moaning as his hands grip me tighter, showing me how much he's enjoying me.

This has butterflies filling my stomach and my mind racing all over the place, wondering what in the hell I'm doing.

Before I can get too lost in him, I work my way out of his arms and toss the money down on the bar, before backing away through the crowd.

I don't make it far, before I feel a firm grip on my waist, as Kash's body slides in behind me.

Why the hell does this have to feel so good?

"I don't want your money, Eden," he whispers against my ear.

"It's not." I stop walking and close my eyes when I feel his hands brush my hair away from my ear. "It's yours. I can't accept your tip. I didn't even earn it. I'm giving it back."

I feel him smile against my ear, causing me to swallow. "Yes, you did. You took the time out of your night to help me out when I needed it. You could've said no to sticking around that night for me."

"No, I couldn't." I shake my head and remove his hand from my waist, before turning around to face him. I'm sure this will be enough to scare him off. "I have a son to take care of, Kash. It was you that was helping me out, but I can't accept money I didn't earn. I should go."

He looks me over for a quick second, before catching my arm when I try to leave. "How old is your son?"

I give him a small smile, not expecting him to care enough to ask me any questions. Most guys would be running the other way at just the mention of me having a kid. "He's five. I should really get back to him. He's with the babysitter and . . ."

His face lights up as he listens to me talk. "He's one lucky little guy to have you." His eyes stay on mine as he speaks again. "Let me take you out on a date, Eden. Let me take care of you for a night and show you what it feels like to go out with a real man."

I don't say anything. Honestly, I'm not sure what to say. All I know is that I could get myself into deep trouble with this man if I don't get out of here soon.

So, I just smile and back up through the crowd, before he can try to stop me again.

As soon as I make it past the security guard and outside, I walk straight over to my jeep and fall against it with a huge smile.

Something about the look in Kash's eyes when I mentioned my son and he asked me to go out with him, tells me he's genuinely interested in me and not just getting laid.

I've been asked out on a few dates in the six months since I've been single and every single one ended up being disastrous, with the asshole assuming he was going to take me to bed at the end of the night and satisfy his own needs.

They never once asked me about my son or what's important in my life. It was obvious they weren't looking for anything deeper than a one night stand.

That's not my style. I need a selfless and caring man that is

serious about a relationship and willing to put my child before
even my own needs.

I know without a doubt that it won't be easy to find and I'm
not sure if Kash can be that guy or not.

Right as I get ready to get into my jeep to head home, I hear
heavy footsteps coming up behind me, before I feel a hand grip
my arm and pull me back with force.

"What the hell are you doing here, Eden?" Knight's angry
voice booms beside my ear as he turns me around and presses
my back against my vehicle. "I went to the house to see *my* son
to find out you were at a fucking male strip club. What gives you
the right to go out and leave Alec with someone else?"

"Let go of me, Knight," I growl out, while yanking my arm
out of his reach and tensing my whole body. "I've been gone for
exactly thirty-five minutes. You're gone every fucking day and
night. Don't you come at me thinking you have the right to tell
me what I can or cannot do. *My* son was already asleep before I
even thought about stepping out that door. So, back off."

"Tell me what the fuck you're doing here!" His nostrils flare
out in rage as he backs me against the jeep again and closes me in
so I can't move. "Who were you with?"

I attempt to push him away, but it doesn't even budge him.
"Let me go, Knight."

He pushes me harder, his body hurting mine. "Answer me!
Who the fuck were you with?"

"Me."

We both look over to the sound of Kash's deep voice as he
comes stalking toward us, looking pissed and ready to strike.

"Don't touch her like that. Take your fucking hands off her
before I remove them my damn self."

Knight lets out a small laugh as if he's amused by Kash bark-
ing orders at him. It's not something he's used to. "You're telling

me what to do with the mother of my child?"

"Damn straight I am." With that Kash pulls him away from me and roughly slams him against the vehicle next to mine, holding him down by his neck. "You never fucking handle a woman like that, motherfucker. Got it?"

"Get the fuck off me." Knight pushes Kash away just enough to take a swing at him, but misses.

This has Kash swinging out, knocking Knight right back against the vehicle and holding him down by his neck again.

Before Knight can manage to attempt to fight back again, two security guards are pulling them apart, wrestling with them to hold them back from each other.

"Calm down, Kash," one of them says, while blocking him with his huge frame. "This is not the time or place for this to happen. Settle it somewhere else."

Kash runs his hands over his face and backs away from the security guard, before turning to face me. "You left this on the bar." He walks up to me and gently grabs the back of my neck, while slipping the tip money into my front pocket. "Riley gave you my number. Promise me you'll call me if that asshole *ever* handles you that way again. Got it?"

Looking him in the eyes, I nod my head, while fighting to calm my racing heart.

Then before I know it, Kash has us turned around so that he's blocking me from Knight as if he's still trying to protect me, even though there's no way he's getting to me again.

Knight is in the background struggling to get past the security guards, his face covered in blood from when Kash punched him in the nose.

I've never seen anyone stick up to Knight like that in the seven years I've known him.

I have no idea what could've happened, but I'm relieved it

got stopped before it could go any further.

Both of these men are powerhouses.

"Go home and lock the door. Lane and Kass won't let your asshole ex leave until you're safe in your jeep and have enough time to get home." His hand comes down to gently run over the red spot Knight was gripping. "Actually, fuck that. I'm driving you home myself."

"You don't have to do that. I'm fine. He won't bother me anymore tonight."

"I want to be positive. I won't stop worrying until I know for sure." He turns away from me to yell over to the security guards who are keeping Knight at a far distance. "Tell Cale I'll be back. I have something important to do real fast."

With that, he gently grips my waist and guides me over to the passenger seat of my jeep, before jumping into the driver seat.

"Give me your keys."

This man really knows how to make a woman's heart beat right out of her damn chest.

He's dependable, caring and protective. Everything Knight isn't . . .

KASH

THE SECOND I WALKED OUTSIDE to see that asshole handling Eden with force, I was ready to rip his throat out with no questions asked.

That kind of shit works me up and pushes me past my boiling point like nothing else.

I will not stand for that shit and my heart is still racing from rage, everything in me wanting to kill that son of a bitch for touching her.

He's lucky she's safe in the car with me and that Kass and Lane were there to pull my ass off. There's no telling how far it would've gotten and I would've hated Eden having to witness the violence.

Without hesitation, I reach over and grab Eden's hand, pulling it into my lap, this need to comfort her taking over.

I feel a slight tug from her as if she's not sure she wants me holding her hand, but the moment, I rub my thumb over her hand, it relaxes in my lap.

"Has he ever put his hands on your son?" I ask the question, not giving a shit if it's crossing the line.

I need to know this in case I see that fucker again. I have no problem sending him a bigger message than I did tonight.

"No," she says quickly. "Of course not. I'd kill that son of a bitch myself if that ever happened and he knows it. He'd never be allowed near either of us for as long as he's breathing."

I relax a bit. "And what about you? Has he ever hit you? Please, don't lie to me either. I know how men like him are. He didn't give a shit about holding you against your will back there."

It's quiet as she lets out a small breath and leans her head back into the seat. "If you mean swinging at me, then no. If you mean him holding me against the wall or dragging me into him and holding me there, then I can't say no about that. He's a possessive man and he's used to getting what he wants."

"Fucking piece of shit." Anger boils up in me, causing me to squeeze her hand and pull it further into my lap as if to protect her, even though he's not around. "And he still wants you?" That thought for some reason pisses me the hell off.

"In some ways . . . yes. We were together for seven years. He had it in his crazy mind that I'd never leave him. That I would stick around and put up with him cheating on me and never being home to help me take care of our child." She pauses for a second and then turns to face me, her hand squeezing mine this time as if she's the one getting angry now. "He expects me to still have sex with him and only him even though we're not together. He's a delusional asshole and we were never meant to date. I was young and stupid. Knight Stevens is a prick."

I thought that asshole looked familiar. I've seen him fight before. Should've known it was him as soon as I heard Eden call him Knight. It's not a very common name, but Stevens is what I know him by.

And she's not wrong. He's a fucking prick.

"So, let me get this shit straight?" I flex my jaw and fight to keep my cool before she really sees how angry this son of a bitch has me. "He goes around fucking any woman he wants and expects you to sit around and wait for him to come take you however and whenever he wants as if he owns you?"

"Like the asshole that he is. You would think Knight would know by now that I won't play by his games. I'm not that girl and never have been." She pulls her hand from mine and points out the window. "Turn left at the next block and go five houses down and it's on the right side."

I grip the steering wheel and do as she says, stopping in front of a small brick house.

I'm so worked up right now, that I just sit here in silence, gripping the steering wheel and flexing my jaw as she looks me over.

I hope like hell now that I get to fight him in a couple weeks, come the big fight.

"Thank you for driving me home, Kash. That was really nice of you." She smiles when I reach over and undo her seatbelt. "Want to take my jeep back to the club and I'll get a ride to pick it up tomorrow?"

I shake my head and turn my gaze to meet her eyes. They're so damn beautiful and full of passion and I have no doubt I'll be picturing them and wondering about her after I leave. "No. I need to get some air."

With that, I jump out of the jeep and walk over to her side, opening the door right as she attempts to.

She gives me a surprised look and smiles as I close the door behind her. "I really appreciate you caring enough to stick up for me. There's not a lot of guys out there like you."

I smile slightly and gently grip the back of her neck, before

I lean in close to her ear. "I know . . . and I'll never be like the asshole you're used to. I'm different, Eden. I'm not afraid to show you that."

My breath against her ear has her shivering in my arms, before she finally grabs for her keys and pulls away, taking a step back.

We both just stand here looking at each other, until I finally speak again. "You have my number. Text me so I have yours."

She nods her head and begins backing away to her house. I can sense the hesitation, as if she wants to ask me in, but knows she shouldn't. "I think I can do that. Especially after what you just did for me."

"Was hoping you'd say that." Taking a chance, I grab her face and press my lips close to hers, hoping like hell it gives her something more to want later. The way she trembles slightly as I pull away shows me she likes my mouth so close to hers. "Goodnight."

Smiling, she clears her throat and begins backing up. "Goodnight, Kash."

I stay here, leaning against her jeep as I watch her disappear into the house and close the door.

After about fifteen minutes, I take off jogging, making my way back to the club.

If that asshole was going to show up and cause trouble tonight, he would've done it by now, wanting to hand me my ass for attacking him.

Maybe that means he's smart enough not to cause trouble near his child.

That's the only thing I can admire about this piece of shit.

Everything else I've heard about him makes me want to teach his ass what it's like to be a real man.

By the time I make it back to the club, Kass is standing at

the front by himself, smiling as he watches me fight to catch my breath.

"Your ass ran back to the club? How far does she live?"

I push past him. "About eight miles."

"Well fuck. That's a good guy there. Got your hero pants on and shit."

I laugh a little and keep on walking, making my way inside and back behind the bar.

"Thanks for deciding to join us again. I'm sweating my ass off back here. Where have you . . ." Sara jumps down my throat but quickly laughs at me once she sees me covered in sweat. "Alright then. Should I ask you what happened?"

I shake my head and quickly jump back into taking orders to give Sara a break. "I'd rather you don't. Not unless you want me breaking bottles against the wall by the end of the night."

"Gotcha. Won't ask."

If I even think about that asshole handling her like that again, I'll lose it all over again and not be able to function the rest of the night.

This run was exactly what I needed to cool off some.

The only thing that will make me cool off even more is if I get a text from Eden, taking me up on that date.

Or hell. Even to just let me know that asshole doesn't show up at her place tonight.

I just hope like hell she uses my damn number . . .

chapter NINE

Eden

IT'S BEEN TWO DAYS SINCE Kash drove me home from the club and I have yet to hear from Knight, surprisingly.

Not that it's unusual to go days without him calling to speak to our son, but after what happened in the parking lot, I expected Knight to show up at my door and jump down my throat about Kash.

There's a huge chance he's embarrassed and that doesn't happen very often. There's not one person I know that is brave enough to attack Knight.

As much as I hate violence, I have to admit that Kash being brave enough to stick up for me was a complete turn on and has only left me thinking about him more.

The way he rubbed me. The way he held my hand. But most of all, the way he kissed me.

His lips so close to mine and so damn soft and tempting. I'd be lying if I said it didn't make me weak in the knees.

I've been so close to calling him, but every time I get ready to hit that button, I think about Alec and how complicated it could get having another man in my life.

"Mommy," Alec's tired voice has me looking over the couch to see him standing there in his Star Wars underwear with his hair standing up all over the place.

"Come here, baby." I wrap my arm around him as he jumps onto the couch and cuddles against my side. "What are you doing up so late?"

He shrugs and wraps his little arm around my mine. "I don't know. My eyes opened up I couldn't stop them. Now I'm not sleeping."

I laugh a little and look down at him. "Why are you so handsome?"

He yawns. "Because I am."

It's the same response I get every time and it never fails to make me smile.

"Close your eyes. It's late. I'll wake you up when it's time to go to Hannah's."

By the time I look down again, he's already sleeping hard against me as if he was never awake in the first place.

My heart swells as I run my hands through his thick hair and watch him sleep.

This little boy will always be the best part of me. Alec is my life. I just wish his father felt the same about him.

The longer I'm awake flipping through channels, the stronger the urge to text Kash gets.

He's most likely at the club and even that isn't enough to weaken my urge to talk to him. Usually, I would never even consider giving a guy with his job choice a shot, especially after dealing with Knight and his late nights out with the crazy women that crowded his fights.

But I can't get over this feeling that is haunting me and

telling me he's different. This feeling that I need to get to know him.

"It can't hurt anything," I finally tell myself. "What's one text? Just one little text?"

Reaching beside me for my phone. I scroll to Kash's number and type out a short message.

> *Eden: I just want to thank you again for what you did for me. I really appreciate it.*

Once I hit send, I set my phone down again, not expecting an instant response. So when I get one, I'm surprised.

My heart speeds up with excitement as I open the message and read it.

I definitely wasn't expecting this kind of reaction out of myself just from receiving a text back from Kash, but clearly, I like him more than I admit to myself.

> *Kash: I'd do it again in a heartbeat, Eden. How's your son?*

His response has my stomach filling with butterflies and me smiling so hard that it hurts. Kash is definitely proving to be different than I expected.

> *Eden: He's a hyper little guy, full of energy and life. I guess you can say he's great. He always is . . .*

> *Kash: Sounds like me when I was a kid. Hell, my ass is still hyper and full of energy. The kid like to play ball?*

> *Eden: More than you know. That and video games. His two favorite things.*

> *Kash: Sounds like my kind of kid.*

Kash: What about you? Are you doing good?

Kash: I'm still available for that massage if you're in need of relaxing . . . I promise to behave as long as you want me to.

I lay back and smile as I read over his texts. He knows exactly what to say to get to my heart and make me laugh at the same time.

There's a huge chance I may begin to enjoy these texts with Kash a little too much.

Eden: Yes, I'm fine. And are you sure about that?

Kash: About what?

Eden: That you'd behave if I want you to.

Kash: I'd do anything you want me to, Eden.

If my heart wasn't racing like crazy, it for sure is now. I'm not sure if texting him was a good idea or if what I'm about to agree to is, but I can't help but want this right now.

This man has a way of making me want things and I kind of like it. No . . . I do like it.

Eden: My father wants to take Alec tomorrow night for a sleepover . . .

Kash: I'll get off work early then. Expect me around nine.

Kash: What about Knight? Did he come over after I left?

Eden: Nope. All is good.

Kash: That's what I was hoping to hear.

Grinning like a damn teenaged girl, I set my phone down and close my eyes, getting comfortable on the couch.

I have to be up for work in five hours and I have a feeling it's going to be close to impossible to fall asleep now.

As much as I may try to downplay my excitement about tomorrow, there's no denying that Kash has me feeling all kinds of giddy right now.

I haven't felt this excited since high school and I love it . . .

KASH

I'VE BARELY BEEN ASLEEP FOR four hours, when the alarm on my phone goes off, causing me to roll over and blindly slap at the bedside table for it.

By the time I get my phone in my hand, I hear Colt throwing things at his bedroom wall, yelling at me to shut the damn thing up before he chokes me.

I get pleasure in his misery, so I lay back and smirk, allowing my alarm to go off in my hand a few more times, before finally shutting it off.

He's part of the reason I couldn't fall asleep last night, thanks to him coming home drunk and horny, fucking Harper against every surface in this damn house.

The other reason was that I couldn't stop thinking about tonight and seeing Eden, but shit, Colt made it worse.

He knows more than anyone that I have a schedule in the morning I've been keeping up with for the last six months. Every Monday and sometimes on Friday.

I haven't broken it yet and I don't plan to now, not even if I didn't sleep for dick and my whole body aches from my performance last night.

"You have no idea how much I hate your ass right now." Colt appears in my doorway, half-naked, running a hand over his sleepy face. "It's like seven. Don't you ever sleep? Shit."

I jump up and reach for the closest pair of jeans and slip them on with a smile. "Nah, I have somewhere to be. Someone's depending on me. Sleep can wait."

Colt closes his eyes and falls against the wall with a grunt. "I don't know how the fuck you do it, man," he says through a yawn. "I'm going back to bed. I don't plan on waking up before seven *tonight* so have fun doing whatever the fuck it is you do this early."

"Good. You're going to need the energy tonight because I'm getting off early. It'll just be you and Myles for the last half of the night."

"Whatever. More money for my ass. Myles can't keep up for shit."

"Better teach his ass to then. He needs to prove himself before Cale replaces him."

"Yeah. Yeah. I'll work with him."

"Better work hard because if he has to bring Styx back, he'll be enough to replace you both. I don't think you want that."

"Hell no I don't. I'm not losing my job over Myles. I got him in so I'll do what I have to do to keep him in."

After Colt disappears, I throw on a t-shirt and my favorite hoodie, before rushing out the door and jumping into my truck.

I'm already five minutes behind schedule at this point, so I take the fastest route to the diner and place my usual order, before rushing out the door.

A satisfied smile takes over as I pull into my sister's driveway five minutes before eight and throw my truck into park.

"Shit, I'm getting good at this little routine."

Jogging up to the front door, I hold the plastic bags with one hand and reach for my sister's key, pushing the door open.

It's quiet, so I walk in and set the bags down on the counter, pulling out the Styrofoam containers and letting the smell of breakfast wake them up.

Just as expected, Alec comes rushing into the kitchen jumping with excitement when he sees me fixing him a plate of blueberry pancakes and fruit. "You brought me pancakes again! I must be good. I know I been. Hannah and my mommy says so."

"Good job." I laugh and walk over to the fridge to pour him a glass of milk. "I can't miss bringing you pancakes, lil man? Plus, I heard you have a new video game to show me so I got here as quickly as I could. Didn't want to wait until Monday."

He nods his head with excitement and quickly pulls out a chair at the table, pumped up as he bounces in his seat. "I do! I'll eat really fast so we can play. It's so cool!"

His eagerness to show me has me lighting up as I set his food down in front of him and start the pot of coffee for my little sister.

"Where's Hannah? Is she still being a sleepyhead?"

Alec throws his head back and laughs. "Yes. She's a big sleepyhead. Sleepyhead Hannah."

"She always has been but you know what?" I say softly, bending down close to him.

"What," he questions in a loud whisper, while sitting up straight.

"I bet if I ate her pancakes that she'd wake right up and tackle me."

Making as much noise as possible, I dig into the second plastic bag and pull out my sister's food.

Alec's laughter only makes it that much louder. I have no doubt, she'll appear in the kitchen in three, two . . .

"Don't you dare touch my food, Hunter Kash Knight." Hannah grumbles, while making her way over to get some coffee. "I only just fell back asleep after Alec getting dropped off. I'm not sure if I should hug you or strangle you on this lovely Friday morning."

"If I told you I brought you corned beef hash, would you settle for hugging me? I'm still a little sore. You might be able to take me right now."

Her eyes get wide with excitement as she rushes over to the table and reaches to open her food. "You brought me corned beef hash? Oh how I love my big brother."

I shake my head. "Nah, they were out."

"Jerk." She opens the Styrofoam and looks around before pushing my shoulder. "Not cool."

"I'm the only jerk that'll bring you pancakes every week though. Remember that, little sister."

She rolls her eyes. "And I suppose I love you for it. Still tired and annoyed but I guess you're pretty awesome."

"I know," I say with a smirk, before looking over to see Alec's plate almost completely empty. "Whoa, little guy. Take it easy before you give yourself a stomach ache like last week."

He shoves the last bite of pancake into his mouth and jumps up with a quickness, his face a sticky mess. "I'm done! I'm done, Hunter! Come on so we can play! Hurry . . ."

Before I can respond, he's grabbing my hand and dragging me into the living room to play his new video game.

Although Alec usually plays on his DS, Hannah told me she bought a Wii U to make it easier for them to play together.

"Whoa, LEGO Star Wars. I've been wanting to try this game, buddy. You any good?"

He nods his head and jumps down in front of the couch, gripping the controller.

The excitement in his little green eyes has me smiling so big that it hurts. I'm not gonna lie, this little guy can make any shit day seem better. Makes me wish I could stop in and hang out with him every morning.

Since my sister's been babysitting him, I've watched myself change a lot. Alec makes me want a family of my own and that's something that hadn't crossed my mind until he started coming around.

Makes my life seem so damn incomplete.

After an hour of playing with Alec, I set the controller down and stand up, knowing I need to hurry and get to the warehouse to meet the guys. "It's time for me to go, lil' man. I have work to do this morning and I'm already late."

"Do you have to?"

"Yeah, it's part of being a grownup. Adulting isn't any fun, so stay a kid as long as you can. Okay?"

He nods his head and laughs. "Okay. I'll do my best."

"Sounds like a plan, lil' man." I nod my head toward the door. "Come on. I can be a few more minutes late. Only for my best little bud though so don't go telling Hannah."

"I won't! I promise."

Just like every visit, Alec rushes past me to get outside and to my truck. He loves sitting in it, so I always let him pretend to drive me around for a few minutes before I leave.

Once I get outside, he's already standing by my huge truck, waiting on me. I boost him up into the driver seat and close the door, before jogging over to the passenger side and getting in.

"Don't drive too fast, bud." I laugh as he turns the wheel to the left, making really loud sound effects. "Whoa! Watch out."

"Don't worry," he says. "I turned just in time."

I almost lose track of time, until Hannah comes out and opens the driver side door. "Alright, buddy. Let's get you cleaned up and dressed."

"Oh man . . ." He throws out his bottom lip. "I want to drive some more. Can I?"

"Sorry." I rub his little head, messing up his hair, before jumping out of the truck to lift him out. "I've gotta get going." Kneeling down in front of him, I pull a baseball out of my hoodie and hand it to him. "How about next week we play a little ball? It's been a while."

"You got me a new baseball?" He smiles, while looking it over with big eyes. "I like it!"

"I knew you would. Now why don't you run in and get cleaned up for Hannah. You gotta do that first before you play your game again. Okay?"

He nods. "Okay! I'll get nice and cleaned up for Hannah."

Hannah smiles as Alec rushes off into the house in a hurry to get cleaned up. "One day, you're going to make a good as shit dad."

I smile, while jumping into my truck, and closing the door behind me. "That's my goal, Hannah Lou Knight."

"Ugh! Don't ever call me by my full name again. I still have no idea what our parents were thinking when they named us."

"Hey, speak for yourself. My name is pretty badass."

"Yeah, alright *Kash.*" She rolls her eyes. "Don't you have someplace to be?" A small cocky smile forms on her lips. "Tell Abe hi for me."

I shift the truck into reverse and laugh. "His ass still whines and cries over you dumping him last year. Maybe you should *stop* having me say hi for you. Yeah?"

"That's what he gets for being a dumbass. So no, I won't stop saying hi. I'll say hi every single day just to remind him what he lost. Let him suffer. Keeps me sane."

I shake my head, amused by my little sister as usual. "I'm out of here. Call me if you need anything."

"Yup! Will do, big brother."

By the time I make it to the warehouse for training, Abe and Calvin are sitting outside the door, looking wide awake and ready to work.

I can't help but to smile at the fact that the guys are taking this shit more seriously now.

Too bad I have to ruin poor Abe's day with this . . .

"Hannah says hi."

"Oh come on," Abe whines, while tossing down his cigarette and stomping it out. "Why does your sister insist on ripping my heart out every damn day? It's been like seven months now and that shit still kills me."

Calvin laughs and slaps his back. "Because you were the dumbass that forced her to break up with you because you weren't *ready* for a commitment. Sucks being an immature guy that doesn't know what he wants, until it's gone doesn't it?"

"Hell yeah, it does."

We all laugh at Abe's misfortune as we make our way inside and begin setting up for the day.

There's no denying the fact that it's going to be a long ass day and night, between training and dancing, but luckily, it's starting out good so far.

I just hope like hell it can stay this way until my time with Eden is over tonight.

We're here for about two hours when my phone goes off in my pocket, distracting me.

Closing my eyes, I take a few deep breaths and release them before swinging at the heavy bag in front of me one last time, then walking away to grab for my water.

After I catch my breath, I lean against the wall and pull out my phone, happy as hell when I see Eden's name across the screen.

Eden: I don't know what it is but ever since you came into my room that night, no one has been showing me their balls. Do I have you to thank?

I find myself laughing at our conversation that night. One of the first things she did was thank me for not showing her my balls. You won't get that from many women.

Kash: I might've asked Riley to pass on a message to anyone working the front desk. There's now a 'no balls' rule. Any guy that comes in has to sign a form.

Eden: I guess I should admit how great you are? Thanks for making my day. My eyes have never been happier.

Kash: Admitting how great I am would make my day. Then we can be even . . .

Eden: You're amazing! Gotta go.

I stand here and stare at my phone, smiling like a dumbass, until Abe pulls me out of it.

"Stop daydreaming little a girl and let's train."

I barely know this woman and she's already got me all wrapped up in her. Now, I need to work on getting her all wrapped up in me . . .

chapter ELEVEN

Eden

MY DAD PICKED UP ALEC thirty minutes ago, and I've been running around the house like a crazy person in attempt to clean it up ever since.

Not that I intend to invite Kash in–it's definitely too soon for that–but it's the first time in weeks that I've had a few moments to get some work done, without Alec zooming around the house like a madman, wanting me to play with him.

I love that kid with everything in me, he's the very reason I breathe, but I've never met a messier or more energetic child in my life.

He definitely takes after his father when it comes to both of those qualities and needless to say, it's exhausting sometimes.

I have to admit that the idea of Kash taking me out tonight–and wanting to take care of me–sounds like a dream come true right now.

I'm so used to taking care of everyone in my life, and putting myself last, that maybe he's right. I deserve just *one* night to have someone else take care of me for once.

Maybe I just want a chance to know what that feels like and I have a feeling that Kash is the perfect guy for just that.

I'm lost in my thoughts, just getting ready to bend down and pick up a stray sock, when the living room door opens to someone letting themselves inside.

My chest immediately tightens with stress, because I know without a doubt that it's Knight letting himself inside, without permission, as usual.

Out of all the nights he chooses to randomly stop in and most likely cause trouble, why tonight?

Damn you, Knight for ruining everything.

"Alec," he yells, while walking through the living room. "Come here, buddy. I got you something."

Shaking my head, I step into the living room and watch as he drops his jacket on the couch. "He's not here. And can you please start knocking? You don't live here anymore. Remember?"

Just as I think he's about to yell at me for Alec not being here, he tosses a small package onto the couch and pulls some flowers out from behind his back.

My stomach instantly twists into knots as his sad eyes meet mine. I automatically know where this is headed. He's good at playing people and making them feel bad for him.

Well not me. Not anymore.

"What are you doing?" Not wanting to deal with the little breakdown that I know is coming, I back up and run my hands over my face. "I can't do this again. Not tonight, Knight. Please don't."

He flashes me that smile that I once found charming and holds the flower arrangement out to me. "Come on, Eden. Don't you stand there and fucking tell me you don't miss me, baby? We both know that's a big lie."

When I still refuse to grab for the flowers, he finally sets them down on the counter himself, before walking over to stand behind me.

My body stiffens from the feel of his arms wrapping around me from behind. Nothing about this feels right or good. "I didn't like seeing you with another man, Eden," he whispers against my ear. "You've been mine since high school. You're still mine. Never forget that."

"No . . . No, I'm not." With force, I break my way out of his arms and point at the door. "I'm not doing this with you. Leave. Please, just leave."

"Come on . . ." Not giving up, he comes back at me, pulling me into his huge arms again. The feel of his lips against my neck has me feeling sick. Who knows how many women those lips have been on. "Alec isn't here. It's just the two of us so stop putting on that tough show and pretending you don't still think about me."

"Knight . . ." I grip his arm and pull it down as he reaches up to grip my breasts. I *hate* the feeling of him touching me sexually. Makes me want to throw up. "It's not a damn show, asshole. I don't want you anymore so stop."

"What the fuck!" he screams, while pushing me away from him. "Who was that guy at the club then? Are you fucking him? Don't fucking lie to me either because you know I'll find out the truth."

"He hasn't been around Alec and that's *all* you need to know. The rest isn't your damn business." I point at the door again, making it as clearly as I can that I want him gone. "Now go. Now."

"Have you fucked him?" he questions again. "I'm not leaving until you answer my damn question and we both know it."

"No! I'm not sleeping with anyone. Now go."

"Fine." He smirks, going back to the cocky asshole I've learned to hate so much. "I have shit to do anyway, but don't think for one second that I won't be back for you and Alec. You're still *my* family. This new guy has another thing coming if he thinks he can steal you guys from me."

"Just go," I growl out. "Right now. Get out."

Relief washes through me as he turns around and leaves, without further argument.

With him, you never know what to expect.

If he's in a certain mood, then nothing you can say or do can get him to go away, but luckily, he probably has one of his sluts waiting on him.

I mean, what is Knight without his group of desperate women up his ass, looking to get laid by a *somewhat* known fighter?

This is not the night to deal with this mess.

Knight is the last person I want around tonight, before seeing Kash. Not to mention that he should be here any second now for our date and they could've bumped into each other.

Having them here at the same time would've been bad news for sure.

After seeing what they're both capable of, with no one here to stop them, who knows what could've went down.

Just as I get a second to catch my breath and recover from Knight's little unexpected visit, the sound of Kash pulling into the driveway has my stomach filling up with butterflies.

I need this date more than ever now. Anything to get the bad taste of Knight out of my mouth and to forget about him touching me.

I find myself smiling as I look through the screen door to see Kash running up to the porch, tossing a baseball up and down in his hand.

He's looking so damn handsome tonight, dressed in a pair of

dark jeans and a fitted button down shirt with the sleeves rolled up to just below his elbows.

The sexy smile on his face and the way his eyes look me over with admiration has my heart going crazy with excitement.

"Are we playing ball tonight?" I nod at the ball in his hand. "It's been a while since I've played with someone over the age of five."

"Me too." He smirks and tosses the ball up once more, before catching it and holding it out to me as I step outside. "I brought it for your son, but I'd be down to play anything you want, Eden. Just as long as I get to take care of you afterward."

"Is that so?" I take the ball from his hand with a smile. "Happen to have an extra ball in that truck of yours?"

He laughs as if it's a silly question. "Oh of course. Never leave home without some."

"I think I might like you even more now." I toss the ball up and catch it, feeling pretty damn enthusiastic about playing ball with Kash. It's a beautiful night to be outside. "I'll put this inside for Alec."

Kash's eyes widen, but quickly goes back to normal as if I was just imagining it.

Who knows . . . maybe I was. It's been a long day.

"That's a good name." He smiles. "So much better than Bob, George, or Kenneth. For a bit there, I was worried for your son's reputation."

Laughing, I push his chest, my eyes widening when it doesn't even cause him to budge. He's rock solid. Even harder than Knight. "Someone spend a lot of time at the gym or is that just from all that erotic dancing and stage humping you do?"

"Both." He flashes me the sexiest grin and reaches behind me to open the screen door. "Toss that inside so I can have fun with you."

Keeping my eyes on him, I toss the ball inside and watch as he locks the door and closes it for me.

"Where are we going?"

He opens the door to his huge truck and boosts me up by my ass, making my heart jump from the firmness of his touch. "To play baseball, of course. And if you're lucky . . . to get a naked massage from me later."

His face stays serious as he leans across me to buckle my seatbelt.

"What makes you think I want a naked massage from you?"

He's still leaning across me, his minty breath hitting my lips, as he speaks. "Are you saying you don't?"

He smirks, when I don't respond, as if he already knew what the answer would be. "I thought so."

With that, he closes the door and hops into the driver side, a satisfied smile on his face as he drives off.

Oddly enough, that has me smiling too.

I like Kash. I really, really do . . .

chapter
TWELVE

KASH

AS MUCH AS I TRY not to think too hard about the fact that
Eden's son's name is Alec, I know without a doubt that it's the
same Alec I've been spending time with at my sister's house for
the last six months.

It has me feeling extremely nervous, but I'm doing everything I can right now not to ruin this night for Eden and give her
a reason to back out of our date.

Hannah told me when she first started babysitting that it
was for a single mother, but I had so much shit going on at the
gym and the club that her name slipped my mind.

I feel like a complete idiot now.

But to be honest, the idea of Alec being her son only makes
me feel more connected to her, drawing me even closer to her
and giving me more reason to want to get to know her.

It sure as shit doesn't scare me away. I'm not like most men
who run at the idea of taking care of another man's child, and
knowing that it's a child I care about; there's no way in hell I'm

backing down from her now.

But I know without a doubt that she'd push me away if she knew I've been spending time with her son and becoming close with him.

Eden is extremely protective of Alec, afraid he'll get hurt again. Just like his asshole father hurt him and I don't blame her.

It's easy to see how much she cares about the little guy. I don't need her telling me she's afraid to let another man in to know.

That's exactly why I'm taking it slow when it comes to learning about her son, not wanting to push it and make her feel uncomfortable.

The last thing I want to do is scare her off before I even get a chance to show her the real me.

When the time is right, I'll bring it up.

"Everything okay over there?" she asks in a soft voice.

I reach over and grab her hand, pulling it into my lap. "It's perfect since you agreed to spend time with me. Was hoping you wouldn't run from me for a third time."

I catch her smile from the corner of my eye, her face turning bright red. "Who says hanging with me is even enjoyable? I could be extremely boring and doing you a favor by running. Never know."

"Nothing about you is boring, Eden." I laugh and pull her closer to me, wanting her to feel how excited I am to be with her. "Trust me."

Her eyes widen, her face turning a deeper shade of red when she gets a feel of my hardness just an inch away from her hand. I know she can feel my pants bulging out, but I don't want to put her hand there until I know she's ready.

I'm down for having fun and showing Eden a good time, but damn if I want her to want it just as bad.

"Maybe I still have a little fun in me after all." Her voice is soft and a little breathless. "Shit, Kash. If you're trying to work me up . . . it's working."

"Have you been with anyone other than your ex?" I have to ask, because it seems as if she hasn't touched anyone other than him. I can tell by the sound of her breathing at just being so close to my dick.

"No," she answers, quickly. "He was my first . . . there hasn't been anyone since."

"Fuck Eden . . ." I squeeze her hand in mine, just thinking about being the only other guy to be inside of her other than the father of her child.

I have no idea why that turns me on even more, but fucking shit, I want to be her next.

I want a chance to show her how a real man takes care of a woman and gives her everything she needs, and craves.

"What?" She squeezes my thigh, causing my cock to jerk. "Does that make you want me even more? Knight never did it for me."

I nod my head and grip the steering wheel with both hands, fighting so damn hard to control myself. "You have no idea the things that makes me want to do to you. To give to you." I place my hand over hers again and squeeze. "Especially knowing he never gave you what you deserved. A woman's needs should always come before a man's."

The rest of the drive to the baseball field is spent with me trying my damnedest to keep some kind of restraint.

It's not easy, especially with her hand gripping my thigh, but I need to do it.

A real man knows when a woman's ready and when that time is right; I'll let go of all restraint, holding nothing back.

"Oh look, there's no one here," she says, while jumping out

of my truck and shutting the door behind her.

I quickly jump out after her and reach into the bed of my truck for some balls, a bat and a couple mitts.

"You know . . ." she spins around and faces me, while walking backwards. "I've gotten pretty good over the months, while playing with my son. Just a warning."

I believe it. Alec is damn good at playing ball. I know because I taught him.

"I guess we'll see just how good. But I should warn you . . ."

"Let me guess . . ." she says teasingly, while looking me over. "You play better in the nude."

I laugh and hand her the bat. "I do *everything* better in the nude. Again . . . a proven fact." I arch a brow and grab a ball, tossing it up, before catching it. "But, I was gonna say I hit pretty far. Not sure it'll be a fair game."

She keeps her eyes on me, trying her best to look intimating as she strips her light jacket off and tosses it at the fence with a cocked brow.

Her confidence is pretty damn sexy right now.

"Oh yeah. Let's play a different kind of game them, Mr. Cocky. Show me how good you are when there's a little distraction."

"Okay." I laugh, dying inside to hear what she's about to come up with. "Your rules. Like I said . . . I'll do anything you want."

She lifts a brow and steps around the fence, up to the batter box. "Whoever hits the furthest out of three balls, gets to choose an item of clothing for the other person to take off. The first person down to their underwear, loses."

I smirk while stretching, letting her know, I'm not taking it easy on her. "You do know I strip for a living, remember? Getting me out of my clothes is pretty fucking easy."

"Yes. But a challenge is sort of fun . . . don't you agree?"

She's the one looking cocky now, as if she expects she won't have to take much off.

"More than you know." I undo the top few buttons of my shirt to give me some more wiggle room and walk over to stand at the pitcher's mound. "Game fucking on."

Placing the bat between her legs, she holds up a finger. "One sec . . ." I watch as she messes around behind her back as if she's either loosening or undoing her bra. "You're not the only one who needs a little more wiggle room," she admits with a grin.

"Hey . . . I don't have a problem with that. It's the only thing you're gonna have on by the time this game is through, so you might as well make sure it's comfortable. Ready?"

"I love your confidence," she says with a grin. "It's cute on you." She nods and gets into a batter stance. "I'm ready."

I grin and hold a finger up. "Wait . . . I'm not quite ready yet." Placing the ball under my arm, I slowly undo my shirt and pull it open, making sure she gets a nice view of my chest and abs.

"You play dirty, I see." She shakes her head and puts on a serious face. "Show me what you got, big guy."

"You sure you want me to?" I lift a brow and reach down to unbutton my jeans.

"That's not what I meant!" she yells.

"Oh." I smile. "Just checking . . ."

I catch her gaze zone in on my chest, watching it flex as I prepare to pitch the ball.

"Hey!" I yell. "Eye on the ball."

"Just throw it," she demands, while looking up and pretending she wasn't just staring at my body. "I'm ready."

Keeping my gaze on her, I throw the ball and smile when she misses.

"That was my warm up swing," she says with a small smile. "Don't judge me just yet."

"I wasn't going to blame it on my body or anything . . ." I reach up and catch the ball as she tosses it back. "I swear."

"Good. Because you'd be wrong anyway." She smiles and gets back into position, clearing her throat a few times and fighting to keep her eyes off me. It has my confidence spiking.

After Eden takes all her swings, only hitting one out of three balls, I take a swing, hitting the first ball so far that we just let it go.

"I believe that means I'm the winner of round one . . ." I nod down at her feet. "I'll start out easy so you're not naked within the first two rounds. Lose the sandals."

Surprising me, Eden strips her shirt off with a confidence that has my cock jumping. "I'm not worried, Kash. I won't be naked within two rounds. So don't take it easy on me."

Apparently, she's going to play by her own rules, just not the ones she set for the game.

Holy fuck . . .

I have no doubt she's doing this as more of a distraction than anything. A way to get back at me for screwing up her first three swings.

And seeing as I can't seem to take my eyes away from her perfect breasts; it might just help her at least get my shirt the rest of the way off.

"I've mastered multitasking pretty damn well. I'll prove it in more ways than one, Eden." I say next to her ear as we pass each other to switch places.

You can tell my words have worked her up a bit, because she doesn't seem quite as confident as she prepares for the second round.

She shakes her head. "No talking . . . cheater."

I laugh at her calling me a cheater. "You're the one standing across from me topless, when all you had to lose were your shoes. You want to play . . . so I'm playing."

And apparently, my dick wants to play too, because it's standing at full attention as I take her in, standing across from me in that red, lacy bra.

"Any day now," she taunts. "Who's distracted now?"

I pitch her three easy balls to hit this time, wanting to make sure this game doesn't end too fast. I'm enjoying myself with her way too damn much to let this game be over soon.

I'm actually surprised when she hits the third ball far enough to just let the ball go and use a new one.

It's pretty fucking hot.

Especially the way her breasts bounced as she swung.

Shit . . . how can I play this off?

Fuck it. I won't.

I let myself be distracted as I take my swings, not hitting them far for shit.

Truthfully, I want out of these damn clothes anyway. I want us both naked, our bodies pressed together as I give up my restraint and take her.

I want to feel her warm skin against mine, our sweaty bodies rubbing together as I bury myself deep and make her forget about Knight all together and how shitty he was to her.

I want to erase her memory with any other man, only allowing her to think about me.

Setting my gaze on hers, I pull my shirt off and toss it, before unzipping my jeans and yanking them off too.

This has her pulling her eyes away from mine to scan over my entire body.

"Your turn," I say, not giving her a chance to ask me why I took off two items of clothing instead of one.

She'll find out soon enough . . .

chapter THIRTEEN

Eden

I DON'T KNOW WHAT KASH is *trying* to do to me, but I can tell you what he *is* doing to me.

He's making me want him so damn badly, that it's making me wish I never suggested playing this game with him.

Now I want to run my hands over every hard inch of his body, feeling him beneath my fingertips.

Every time I even look his direction or hear the deepness of his sexy voice, I have to clench my thighs and take a deep breath.

I just wanted to have fun with Kash. For us to run around and laugh and just let loose, be free. Something I haven't done in a while.

I didn't mean for it to turn into me wanting his hard body against me.

All I can think about is him kissing me, our half-naked bodies molded together as his tongue runs along my lips, tasting me.

I'm trying so damn hard not to picture him slamming me against this fence behind me with his body between my legs.

"Any day now . . ." Kash teases with that sexy little smirk of his. "If you think you can focus on the ball, that is."

I clear my throat and point the bat at him. "That's the only thing I'm focused on." I lie.

"I see." His eyes follow mine down to his package as I lose my battle and look down again. "That's not the *balls* you should be focused on, darlin'."

"I can't help it." I laugh and then quickly gather my composure. "It's the white boxer briefs. They're distracting in the dark."

"I know," he responds, cockily. "Why do you think I took my jeans off too?"

"Oh, you ass!" I hold the bat into position, feeling my pulse racing. "So now what happens if I win this round? You have nothing left to take off." I bite my bottom lip, trying to hold back my smile as I watch him tossing the ball up and down.

He grins and snaps the top of his boxer briefs. "Sure I do. If you win . . . I lose the briefs."

My eyes widen, not expecting that answer. "Seriously! You're going to get completely naked . . . out here? What if someone sees you?"

"It wouldn't be the first time I've been nude outside in public, Eden. I've done far worse things than just be *naked* in public. Trust me." He arches a brow, trying to hold back a smile. "Batter up."

He's getting under my skin and he knows it. He's good with that mouth of his, always knowing just what to say to keep my curiosity piqued.

As hard as I try to stay focused on the ball, his confession and those damn underwear keep pulling my attention away, causing me to hit all three balls like crap.

I toss the bat down and meet up with Kash in the middle, smiling as his hand grips my waist. "I should kick your ass for distracting me. That's not even fair."

He smiles and grabs my chin now, causing me to look up at him. "You should," he whispers against my lips. "But we both know it's making you want to kiss me instead."

With that, he releases my chin and walks away, leaving me standing here, breathing heavily.

He's right. I do want to kiss him, but I want *him* to kiss me even more.

And we both know what this next pitch will lead to . . . us both in our underwear, out here, alone, in the night.

The thought has my heart fluttering and my skin burning with need.

"Ready?" I watch as he hits the bat against the dirt and then gets into batter position. Holy shit, this is the hottest thing I've ever seen.

A man playing ball in his underwear.

I'm crazy for suggesting this game with Kash. I'm even crazier for thinking it wouldn't make me want him more than I already do.

Taking a deep breath, I slowly release it at the same time I release the ball.

My gaze stays locked on it flying through the air as Kash's bat smashes against it with a loud thud.

I don't even have to look to know I've lost. The look on his face says it all.

"Looks like we'll both be out here in our underwear."

Shaking my head, I undo my jeans and slowly strip them down my legs, feeling excitement course through me at the thought of being out here in just my underwear.

I've never done anything like this before.

"I still say you cheated." I walk over to him and toss my jeans at his face, right as he gets ready to speak.

I can't help but to laugh as he just stands there with a surprised look on his face. "It's like that, huh?"

My breath hitches in my throat as he quickly reaches out and pulls me into his arms, our half-naked bodies molding together as he smiles down at me.

"A little distraction never hurt anyone and I can promise you that you were just as much of a distraction to me as I was to you." He gently rubs his thumb over my bottom lip, before leaning in closer, our lips brushing together. "You've been a distraction since the moment I laid eyes on you, Eden and I've been wanting to do this more than fucking anything."

His lips crash hard against mine, his kiss overpowering, and breathtaking, causing me to hold onto his neck for support.

My hands move up to dig into his thick hair, my heart racing fast against his, as his mouth claims mine, tasting and owning me.

I'm so lost in the intensity of our kiss, that I don't even realize I'm off the ground, until my back is slammed against the fence, his hard body pressed between my legs.

It feels exactly how I imagined. Exciting and extremely hot.

I moan out as he bites my bottom lip and grabs both my hands, holding them above my head, pressed against the fence.

"Hold on . . ." he whispers against my lips.

I grab onto the fence behind me, holding on as tightly as I can, as he lowers his hands down to grip my ass.

The way his hips move against me as he kisses me has me wrapping my legs tighter around him, desperate to feel him hard, against me.

He's so big and so damn stiff.

Pulling away from his kiss, I slam my head against the fence and bite my bottom lip as I feel Kash's hand running down my stomach, teasing me.

The way my body heats up with excitement once it slides down my panties surprises me. I've honestly never been this turned on in my entire life.

"Yes . . ." I nod my head, giving him the okay to go further. "Keep going."

"You sure?" he kisses my neck, before nibbling it. "There's a huge fucking chance that if I touch you the way I want to that we'll both end up naked in the dirt."

I swallow, my whole body reacting to his words. If Kash were any other man, I'd be pushing him away right now, but I don't want to.

I need this. I want this.

It's been too damn long.

"Touch me," I whisper.

As soon as the words leave my lips, Kash's fingers slide between my slick folds, causing me to gasp out.

"Oh shit, Eden." He slams me harder into the fence, his body holding me in place. "You're so damn wet."

His mouth captures mine, hard with desperation, his two fingers pushing into me at the same time.

The feel of him inside of me almost instantly sets me off, so I clench my thighs around him and yank at his hair. "It's been a while, Kash." I pull his hair harder, my body squeezing him tighter as he begins pumping in and out with a sexy little growl. "You're going to make me come . . ."

"That's my goal, Eden." He moves his thumb up to rub my clit as his two fingers continue to pump in and out of me. "I want to feel your tight little pussy clench my fingers as I make you come. Show me how good it feels."

My breathing picks up, my body now feeling as if it's on fire as he picks up speed, making me feel a sensation I've never felt before.

My body is on the verge of exploding right here in Kash's strong arms and I don't feel one bit of shame or regret. All I feel is need. A need to let him take care of me.

It's when I feel his thick cock press against my ass as he grinds his hips into me that my orgasm sweeps through me, making me scream out in pleasure as my pussy clamps around Kash's fingers.

"Kash! Oh shit . . . oh . . ." I grab onto the back of his neck and hold on tightly as I ride out the intense wave of pleasure.

A smirk takes over Kash's face as he waits for my orgasm to stop, before finally pulling his fingers out and sucking them clean with his mouth.

"Fuck . . . Eden." He licks his lips as if making sure to get every last drop of my taste from his mouth. "You taste fucking fantastic."

I don't know what to say, so I just bury my face into his neck and smile, while trying to catch my breath.

"I don't think this is the right kind of massage you promised me . . ."

He cups my face, making me look up at him. "This isn't even half of what I promised you, Eden. I want to give you so much more and I will . . . soon."

"Hey!"

We both look over at the sound of some teenager's voice. "You guys having sex over there or can we play some baseball?"

"Oh shit." I cover my face and laugh, happy that we didn't end up, naked in the dirt. "We should go."

"Give us a minute, man." Kash grins and sets me back down to my feet, doing his best to keep my body covered. "You get dressed first. I could give a shit if these kids see me in my underwear."

Rushing to reach for my clothes, I cling onto Kash, trying to keep a straight face as I get dressed.

I would think that I'd be embarrassed right now, but surprisingly I'm not.

Knowing that Kash is in this with me and I'm not alone, has me smiling and feeling . . . free.

Once I get my clothes on, I grab his shirt and jeans and start walking to the truck, looking behind me to see him following me with a huge grin.

There's now a group of six teenagers, probably close to eighteen or nineteen years old. Two of them are girls that keep whistling at Kash, showing admiration for his hot body.

Smiling, I toss his clothes into the back of the truck and hop in the passenger seat.

I laugh when Kash leaves his clothes in the back and jumps into the truck in his underwear.

"Good thing I left my keys in the truck." With that he smiles and starts the engine. "And seeing as you like my body so much, I left my clothes in the back where you put them."

"Good." I place my hand on his muscular thigh and squeeze it. "Because I more than like the view next to me right now."

I could stare at this man's body all night . . .

chapter FOURTEEN

KASH

OH FUCK . . .

Eden is making it impossible at this point not to pull this damn truck over and fuck her on the side of the road.

After getting a feel of her tight, wet pussy and how hard it clenched as I made her come, makes me want to pleasure her even more.

I want to feel her clamp hard around my cock as I make her come undone with my body. I want her arousal coating my dick, showing me how good I make her feel.

My muscles flex as Eden moves her hand further up my leg, stopping right next to my hard-on. "Touch it, Eden. It's yours to fucking handle any way you please."

Without a word, she slides her hand where she really wants it. Where we both really want it.

"Mmm fuck . . ." I let out a growl when Eden's hand grabs my cock and squeezes it through the thin fabric.

The little gasp that leaves her lips tells me that she's surprised at how huge it feels in her hand. I'm used to that reaction.

"Shit, Kash . . ." She releases my cock and looks at it with wide eyes. "It feels even bigger than it looks. I'm a little intimidated, to be honest."

"Don't be." I release the steering wheel long enough to grab both her hands and place them on my erection. "Use both hands. I promise you can handle it."

She leans over and kisses my neck with confidence, while pulling my cock out of my boxer briefs and grabbing it with both hands.

"Holy fuck, Eden . . ."

I growl and grip the steering wheel tighter, as she begins stroking my thick shaft with both hands, brushing her thumbs over the head of my cock each time she reaches the top.

I honestly didn't think Eden would let things get as far as they have tonight, which only makes it that much fucking harder not to bust my load all over this truck right now.

She's about to make me lose it with one more damn stroke. I can't handle not being inside her right now.

Fuck . . .

A small breath escapes her as I pull my truck over on a side road and reach over to undo her seatbelt.

"I can't handle this shit, Eden."

I can see her chest quickly rise and fall as her eyes meet mine, waiting for me to make my next move. "Can't handle what?"

"Not being inside you. Not fucking making you come again. Shit . . . not giving you what you deserve."

Keeping my eyes on hers, I grip the side of her face and lean in, crashing my lips hard against hers.

A surprised breath escapes her the moment our lips crash together, her hands reaching around to grip the back of my hair with desperation.

"Kash . . ." she whispers, pulling away slightly.

I grip her tighter and rub my thumb over her bottom lip with a smirk. "You want me to make you come again?" I brush my lips over hers, before growling against them. "I'm trying to take it slow for you, but I have a feeling you need me inside you just as much as I need to be."

She sucks in a quick breath right before my lips slam against hers again, my mouth claiming hers, recklessly.

She tries pulling away after a few seconds, but I bite her lip pulling her back to me. Her mouth tastes so fucking good that I'm not ready to stop yet.

Keeping my mouth on hers, I reach down and push her seat back as far as it goes, before spreading her legs and moving in between them. Her body feels so fucking good beneath mine that I can't help but to be rough, my kisses becoming harder and deeper, giving her a glimpse of how I am in the bedroom.

I'm anything but gentle when it comes to being inside a woman. From my experience, they all want it hard and deep, hitting every fucking spot and I more than deliver.

Eden has no idea the things I can do to her.

Both of my hands tangle into the back of her long hair as she moans into my mouth, before speaking. "I do want this . . . you . . . but . . ."

"Tell me, Eden."

"I'm not sure I'm ready," she admits. "But I want you so damn badly right now. All I can think about it how you'd feel inside me. I haven't wanted a man inside me for a while now but you make me want things, Kash."

I grip the seat around her, trying like hell to keep my cool and prepare to talk my dick down if it comes down to it.

"I'm ready to give you anything you want, Eden. I want you for more than just *this*. But I won't lie when I say I want to fuck you hard and fast right now and show you how a real man takes care of a woman's needs."

She looks down and moans as my cock jerks. "Holy shit . . ."

That's all it takes for me to know she wants this just as badly as I do.

Locking eyes with hers, I undo her jeans and slide them down her legs.

Then I slide my hands up her stomach and grip her shirt, pulling it over her head, stripping her back down to just her bra and panties once again.

When her lips part and a sexy little breath leaves her lips, I lose it and grip her thighs, bringing the head of my cock meet her entrance.

It brushes against her warm pussy, causing her to spread her legs for me and bite her bottom lip with need.

Fuck me . . .

I want to do this. I want to be inside her more than anything, but as soon as her phone vibrates next to us, *"dad"* popping up on the screen, I hesitate, knowing that it's most likely Alec calling her.

If I fuck Eden on our first date, she's going to think I only want her for this reason once it's over. I can't have that shit. I can't have her thinking I don't want to be there in the future for her and her son.

"I'm sorry," I whisper into the side of her hair. "Your son . . ."

She leans forward with a quickness, once she finally notices her phone going off. "Oh shit!"

I instantly see the guilt take over her face as she turns the phone over and looks me in the eyes. "I should get dressed so I can call Alec back. I never miss his call before bed."

Smiling, I cup her face and press my lips against hers, letting her know I understand. "I agree and you shouldn't start now."

Reaching beside me, I grab for her jeans and help her pull them back up her legs.

As she's finishing getting dressed, I run around to the back of my truck and get dressed myself, smiling as a car full of women slowly drive by, honking and whistling at me, while I stand here half-naked on the side of the road.

It's then that I look over to see Eden standing next to my truck, smiling too as I pull my jeans up. "Not sure we would've gotten much privacy here. Those women looked as if they were ready to pull over and join you until they noticed me."

I walk over and grab her waist, pulling her against me to show her I'm focused on her and her alone. "Do you want more privacy next time? I can arrange that."

She leans in and presses her forehead to mine, seeming a bit embarrassed by our situation. "Maybe . . . I don't know. We were two seconds away from having *sex*, Kash. I don't know what I was thinking. I was too wrapped up in you and that's not something I let happen so easily with anyone." With that she kisses my cheek and pulls away from me. "I need to call my son back before he falls asleep."

Giving her some privacy, I jump back into my truck and turn on the radio, letting the whole night replay in my head.

I never have unprotected sex, yet with her, it didn't even cross my mind to search for a condom. It was as if being with her just felt so damn natural. Kissing her, touching her and being inside her was all that mattered when it came down to it.

Pulling me from my thoughts, Eden hops into the truck a few minutes later with a huge smile on her face. "Alec just wanted to say goodnight and tell me how much fun he's having beating grandpa at video games. I love that kid so damn much."

"He sounds like a great kid."

My stomach sinks at the thought of keeping this secret from

her, but I need more time to show her who I am.

We need more time before she gets scared and pushes me away.

"It's getting pretty late . . ." I grab her hand and pull it into my lap. "I should get you home in case Alec calls again because he wakes up."

She squeezes my hand. "Thank you."

I press her hand to my mouth and kiss it. "For what?"

"For understanding . . . for stopping when you saw my phone go off. Not many guys would give a shit."

"Well I do. I give a shit more than you know." I place her hand on my thigh and squeeze it, keeping my hand on hers the whole way to her house.

Pulling up in the driveway, I quickly undo my seatbelt and run over to open the door for Eden.

She smiles, grabbing my hand as I help her down to her feet. "Don't get me too used to this," she says with a laugh. "Then I'll expect it from every guy in the future."

I reach behind her and shut the truck door, before grabbing her face and speaking next to her ear. "Maybe getting you used to *me* is what I want so there won't be any other guys in the future . . ."

I hear the slight sound of her swallow, before she lets out a small breath. "Goodnight, Kash. Thank you for a fantastic night."

"Goodnight, Eden." I place a gentle kiss beside her lips, before watching her disappear into the house.

I have no fucking idea how I'm going to get any sleep tonight after watching her walk away, but I know without a doubt that I did the right thing by not fucking her like I wanted to.

Eden isn't like other women and I need to make sure I show her that . . .

chapter FIFTEEN

Eden

AFTER KASH DROPPED ME OFF last night, I spent the entire night thinking about him and how damn good he made me feel, not just physically but emotionally.

He made me smile and laugh harder than I have in a very long time with anyone other than my son.

Kash has a way of making me feel carefree and full of life, allowing me to let loose and just live for the moment.

I don't seem to worry about all the small things when I'm with him and I know more than ever now that I need that in my life.

I *want* that in my life.

The only thing that scares me when it comes to being around Kash is that I want him *physically* more than any man I've ever met.

When I'm with him all I can think about is him touching me. His sexy lips and hands all over my naked body, making me come undone until I'm screaming out his name.

I want to *feel* every inch of kash. My desire for him almost got me in trouble last night and it was only the first date. I have no idea what I'll allow to happen if I see him again, yet I still *want* to see him again.

I've been awake for almost an hour now, lying in bed, thinking about him and how much I want to spend time with him again.

That says a lot.

"What am I going to do with this man? He's every-thing . . . Ugh . . ."

Rolling over, I smash my face into the pillow, smiling into it as I think about how hard he made me come last night.

Just the memory of him slamming me against the fence with his fingers inside me sets my entire body on fire with this desire I've never felt before.

The way he touched me was unlike anything I'd ever experienced before. It was as if he was taking the time to learn my body and find out exactly what spot would set me off and send my body into an overload of sensations.

It didn't take him long to find what he was looking for and when he found it, he mastered it, completely owning my body until it exploded around his fingers.

Rolling back over, I slide my hand down my panties, needing some kind of release, but nearly jump out of bed when the doorbell goes off.

"Holy fuck!" I throw my hands over my face and shake my head, hoping like hell it's not my father and Alec right now. With the thoughts running through my head seeing them is the last thing I want. "Please be someone else. Please . . ."

Sitting up, I adjust my pajama shorts and jump out of bed, rushing into the living room to look out the window.

My heart drops to my stomach so fast that I almost feel sick when I see whose vehicle is parked outside.

My need to be quick suddenly disappears, causing me to hesitate before I undo the chain lock.

Apparently, that was the only thing keeping Knight out, because as soon as I drop the chain, he's pushing the door open with a scowl.

"Really? Since when do you lock that damn thing?"

Rolling my eyes, I make my way into the kitchen to start a pot of coffee.

Seeing *him* right now only guarantees it'll be a crap day. Nothing good ever comes out of his visits.

"Since you decided to keep letting yourself in without my permission. Dammit, Knight . . . What do you want? You know Alec is at my father's."

"Some alone time with you." He grips my waist from behind, pulling my ass against his erection. His horny little moan beside my ear has my stomach twisting into knots. "Been thinking about you all morning and how good you feel wrapped around my dick, baby. It's been a while."

"Let go." I punch his hand repeatedly until he eventually let's go, allowing me to walk away. "I don't think so. Nope. Not happening."

"Why the fuck not?" he snaps.

I turn around to look at him, letting him see the hatred in my eyes. He's such an asshole. "Because we're not together anymore, that's why. What the fuck, Knight. This needs to stop."

"That shit doesn't matter, Eden. You belong to me still and we both know it."

"The fuck I do." I slam my fist down onto the counter, causing him to grin like an asshole. "I don't *belong* to you, Knight. Never fucking have, but you were too thickheaded to get that. Just leave. There's no reason for you to be here."

Keeping that stupid, asshole grin on his face, he reaches for his shirt and yanks it over his head as if that's all it'll take for me to change my mind. His eyes meet mine as he comes closer to me, reaching for my waist. "I'm so fucking horny right now, Eden."

Me too, asshole. Just not for you . . .

"I'm not having sex with you, Knight. What the fuck is wrong with your head?" I roll my eyes at his chest when he flexes it, thinking it'll have me falling all over him. "Put your shirt back on. It's not working." I slap his hand away when he reaches for me again.

He lets out a confused little laugh. "And what . . . someone else's works better for you?"

"Yes," I say matter-of-factly. "Your chest isn't the best one I've ever laid eyes on so get over yourself and leave."

He grabs for his shirt, and balls up in his fist, pissed off that I find someone else's body more attractive than his. "You talking about that asshole from the club?"

"He's not an asshole," I point out. "But you're being one, as usual. Goodbye, Knight. I don't want you here. Leave. Now."

"Fuck this shit. I have bitches on standby twenty-four seven. You're lucky I'm even here to begin with. Don't you get that? I can do so much better than you."

I laugh at his delusional comment and pour myself a big ass cup of coffee. I need it more now than ever, after dealing with this asshole. "So damn lucky," I say mockingly. "I get to deal with the biggest asshole to walk this earth at . . ." I look up at the clock. "Seven in the morning. How fucking lucky could I be?"

Before I know it, Knight grabs for the entire coffee machine, picks it up and tosses it across the room.

I stand here, sipping on my coffee, trying to give off the impression that he has no effect on me whatsoever.

"You can leave now," I demand.

He growls out and punches the wall, standing in front of it for a few seconds, before speaking. "That little asshole of yours can expect a visit from me at the club. Don't be surprised if he never looks in your direction again. He won't want to after what I plan to do to that pretty little face of his."

This has me losing my composure. Even though I'm sure Kash could handle him, he shouldn't *have* to. "Leave him the hell alone, Knight! Get the fuck out! Now!"

I slam my coffee down next to me and point at the door when he doesn't make a move to leave. "Get. Out." Realizing that he doesn't plan on going; I give him a shove toward the door.

"Get off me, bitch." With one swing, he knocks me down to the ground, before tossing his shirt at my face. "Like I said, we'll see if this asshole still wants you once I'm through with him. I fucking doubt it so don't hold your breath."

With that, he takes off, slamming the door behind him, so hard that the walls shake.

I lay here for a few seconds, fighting to catch my breath from the hard impact of hitting the floor, before I finally sit up.

Carefully, I reach up and touch my face, wincing from the tenderness, before I scramble to my feet and lock the door again, including the chain lock.

This is the last time Knight will be allowed inside. I'm having the locks changed *today*.

This asshole has me worked up completely, feeling shaky and on edge. He's never once laid his hands on me before now. I'm so damn angry that I could cry, but I won't.

I've cried too many times over the years because of that piece of shit.

An overwhelming feeling to talk to Kash hits me, causing me to make my way to my bedroom and grab for my phone.

I'm not sure why but I feel like I need him right now.

Eden: Are you awake?

Ten minutes go by without a response back from Kash. With his late-night work schedule, I expected Kash to be a late sleeper, so I'm not really surprised.

Just disappointed.

I toss my phone down and run my hands over my face, in attempt to calm down and forget about Knight.

I'm tired of feeling helpless when it comes to him. I'm tired of him disrespecting me and thinking he can walk all over me, although I know that won't change anytime soon.

I was his first and he was mine. He planted his seed in me and he'll always think he owns me because of that.

Just as I begin to calm down a bit and clean up Knight's mess, the doorbell rings again.

A whole new wave of stress hits me, causing me to feel sick to my stomach.

I can't deal with Knight again. If I see his face again today, it's going to take everything in me not to punch it.

Setting down the dustpan, I walk over to the window and look outside, praying with everything in me that I don't see Knight's car.

The sight in front of me has all my stress melting away and a small smile taking over.

I need this right now. I need *him* right now.

Looks like Kash is awake after all . . .

KASH

I SHOULD BE AT THE gym right now, meeting up with Styx, but I couldn't start my day without seeing her first.

Eden's been the only thing on my damn mind since I dropped her off last night and to be honest, I can't even remember a time when a woman has had me all twisted up, needing to see her and talk to her.

My thoughts wouldn't let me sleep for shit, so I jumped out of bed at one and hit the bags at the warehouse, needing some time to myself to relieve some tension.

Even after wearing myself out, I still didn't get but maybe two hours of sleep after that.

All I wanted to do was text Eden or just show up at her house but I didn't want to be that asshole who puts my needs first.

I almost allowed that to happen last night in my truck and I won't do that to her again. Not until I know she's ready.

She's worth too much to me and I plan to do what I can to

prove that to her.

Standing on the front porch, I take a deep breath and ring the doorbell, my heart fucking racing with anticipation.

I have no idea how she's going to react to me showing up at her door unannounced, but I hope like hell she wants to see me right now just as much as I want to see her.

If it weren't for the fact that I know Alec is gone, then I wouldn't be here, but he is and I want to do something nice for her.

The door opens and my chest tightens at the sight of her, standing there in a pair of little white cotton shorts and a gray tank top shaking before me.

She's doing her best to hold it together, but there's no mistaking that someone upset her and left her pissed off and shaken up.

I don't wait for her to invite me in. Fuck that. Someone messed with her and I need to know what the hell happened.

Tensing my jaw in anger, I step inside and toss the bag of pancakes down beside me, before reaching out to cup her face in my hands. It's then that I notice her right cheek is red as if someone's just slapped her.

"What the fuck happened? Did Knight hit you?" Rage takes over as I picture him putting his hands on her. "I'll fucking kill him for hurting you, Eden. Where is he?"

She places her hands on mine in attempt to calm me down. "He stopped by about fifteen minutes ago . . . he's gone." Her hands squeeze mine as I run my thumbs over her cheek to comfort her. "He said some things that really got to me and made me lose it. I don't get why I still allow him to get me so worked up but I do. He always knows exactly what to say to piss me the hell off. I shoved him to make him leave and he swung out and knocked me down."

I tense my jaw again, knowing that I'll need to take care of him later for placing his hands on her. Right now, I need to take care of her emotionally. "Tell me what that piece of shit said to upset you."

She releases a breath and kisses my arm as if it's so natural to do. I love that she feels comfortable with me right now, even with seeing how pissed off I am. "He threatened to pay you a visit so you'll stop talking to me. The idea made me lose it."

Pissed off, I close the door behind me and turn us around so that her back is now pressed against the door. "He's mistaken if he thinks there's anything he can do to keep me from you, Eden." I lean in and press my forehead against hers. "I'm already in too deep to let anything fuck that up and scare me away."

She smiles and wraps her arms around my neck, gently pressing her lips against mine, before speaking. "I care about you, Kash." The feel of her lips brushing mine as she speaks, instantly has my cock hard, even though sex is the last thing I should be thinking about right now. "Doesn't mean I expect you to stick around and fight my battles. You shouldn't have to."

"Fuck what I shouldn't have to do. What you make me want to do is what matters to me." I suck her bottom lip into my mouth, gently nibbling it, before I release it. "I'm here for as long as you want me to be. That's no fucking lie, Eden. Let your ex try to run me off. That shit ain't happening."

My words have her breathing heavily against lips as if she wasn't expecting that answer. "You're so different than I expected. It scares me."

I press my body into hers, while reaching down to grip her hips, digging my fingers in with need. "Don't let it."

Her heart is beating wildly against my chest, as her fingers dig into my shoulders, letting me know that she's just as desperate to touch me as I am her right now.

As much as it turns me on; I can't stop thinking about what that piece of shit did to her. The things he fucking said . . . his hands on her.

I need to get to him.

"Fuck . . ." I bury my face into her neck, before trailing my lips up it, stopping at her ear. "Tell me where I can find Knight."

"Kash, that's not a good idea." She releases my shoulders and grabs my hand pulling me through the house with her, until we're in her bedroom. "He's with a bunch of his friends right now. They're all assholes and won't hesitate to jump on his side."

I stand in the doorway and watch as she changes into a small white sundress, before she walks over and kisses my cheek.

Seeing her dressed like this is making it even more impossible to not want her right now, but I need to keep my head where it belongs.

And that's knocking Knight on his ass just like he did to Eden.

Growling, I cup her face and bend down so our lips are close. "I don't care if he has a fucking army with him. Please . . . tell me where this piece of shit is."

She lets out a defeated breath as I bury her face into my chest and rub the back of her head. "A warehouse over on Burrow Street."

I kiss the top of her head and turn around to leave. "I'll be back."

Just as I'm about to pull out of the driveway, I look over at the sound of my passenger door opening.

Eden looks up at me and jumps inside, slamming the door behind her. "I'm not letting you go there alone, Kash. The only reason this is happening is because of me. I hate that."

I close my eyes and take a few calming breaths, needing to do something before I lose it. As much as I hate this son of a bitch and want him to hurt; I can't do what I want to him with Eden around.

With a growl, I reach over and grab Eden's waist, pulling her into my lap so that she's straddling me, our faces almost touching. "I want you, Eden. I'm not gonna let some asshole and his douche friends stop me from getting you. They can't keep me away. I want you to know that."

"I do now," she whispers against my lips. "But I don't want you fighting for me."

I wrap my arms around her neck and pull her further down into me, tensing my jaw at the feel of her body against mine. "Fighting for the ones I care about is what I do. Nothing can stop me from doing that."

Her eyes meet mine and the expression in them tells me just how badly she truly needs me right now.

She needs me just as badly as I need her and this time I know she's ready. I can *feel* it.

Tangling my hands in her hair, I lean in and swipe my tongue over her lips, causing her to close her eyes and moan.

"You're so hard, Kash." She digs her nails into my shoulder and leans her head back. "You feel so damn good beneath me."

I move my hands down her body to grip her waist as I begin grinding my hard cock against her pussy, showing her just how hard I really am. "I'll feel even better inside you."

My words have her body shaking above me as if that's all that's needed in this moment to set her off.

Her lips meet mine, roughly, with a need that has my cock fighting to break free from my denims.

Unable to hold back anymore, I lift her body up and undo my jeans with my free hand, allowing my erection to spring free.

Keeping my mouth on hers, I reach into the glove compartment and pull out a condom, before pulling away and ripping the wrapper open with my teeth.

I keep my right hand wrapped inside Eden's hair as I struggle with rolling the condom on with my left. "Fuck, these things never fit right."

"Forget the condom, Kash," she breathes out in desperation. "I'm on the pill. Shit . . ." She stills for a second as if she's not sure she said the right thing. "I trust you. You've given me every reason to."

"Fuck . . . Eden." My heart jumps around in my chest at the idea of being inside Eden bare. And the thought that she's allowing me to; has me already wanting to come.

I trust her too. So . . .

Digging my teeth into her neck, I push her panties aside with my free hand and slowly push her down onto my cock, us both moaning out as I fill her.

Her wetness coats my dick, letting me know just how turned on she is by me being inside her this way.

"Holy fuck, Eden . . ." I grip her hips with both hands and squeeze. "You ready for me to move?"

She digs her nails into my shoulders and presses her forehead to mine, taking a few deep breaths. "Yes. I'm ready."

Taking control, I lift her up and push her back down, hard and deep, causing her to scream out and bite my shoulder. I don't move too fast though, not wanting to hurt her too much.

I do this a few more times, getting her used to my size, before I begin moving myself, meeting her body half-way with each thrust.

Our bodies are molded together, sweat coating our skins as I continue to move inside her, being sure to hit deep with each move of my hips.

"Kash . . ." she moans into my ear, before biting it. "I've fantasized about this moment since the day you showed up at my work. What it would feel like to have you inside of me . . . filling me."

"Holy fuck, Eden." I grab her shoulders and hold her down on my cock. "Seriously?"

She smiles against my ear before whispering, "Yes. I've touched myself to thoughts of you more times than I can count."

"Fuuuuck." I reach down and push the seat back as far as it can go. "Hold on, baby. It's about to get rough."

I grab the back of her head and slam my mouth against hers, biting her lip to keep her close as I begin bouncing her up and down on my dick so hard that she has to hold onto my shoulders to keep from banging her head on the roof.

Moaning out, I protect her head with my right hand, while holding her hip with my left.

"Kash . . ." she moans out. "I'm about to come . . . fuck . . . ohh-hhh . . . fuck . . ."

"That's good, baby. Come . . . come all over my dick for me."

With a few more hard thrusts, I feel myself close to busting, so I slow down, wanting to make sure she comes before me.

I grip her ass with both hands and squeeze, guiding her body, slow and deep, hitting her where it counts. "I'm coming," she moans out as the same time I feel her pussy squeezing my dick.

"Oh fuck . . ." I feel myself about to lose it from her pussy clenching around me, but throw my head back and tense my jaw, fighting it. "You good?"

She nods her head and presses her lips against mine. "So damn good, Kash. Holy shit . . ."

"Okay . . . good. I'm gonna bend you over the seat now." I pick her up and adjust her how I want her, with her elbows on the passenger seat, her ass facing me. "Dig your nails into my leather if you have to. I'll fucking replace it."

Before she can say anything, I wrap an arm around her waist and grip her hair with my other hand, slamming into her so hard and deep that she screams out and buries her face into the seat.

I continue to fuck her hard just like I'm used to, taking her deeper than I hope that motherfucker has ever been.

I want my dick to erase any memories of that asshole ever being inside of her. I *need* it to feel so damn good that she'll never want anyone other than me again.

Her nails dig into my leather as she screams out my name so loudly that it has me pulling out of her and releasing my load on her ass.

"Fuuuck me . . ." I rip my shirt off over my head and place it on her ass, while fighting to catch my breath. "Shit, Eden. I'm sorry if I hurt you. I can't control myself when it comes to you."

"Good," she says breathlessly. "I don't want you to."

After cleaning her off and adjusting our clothing, I pull her back into my lap and kiss her. "I'm not going anywhere, Eden. I can promise you that sex isn't what I want from you. I want *you.*"

"I know," she says softly. "If I didn't then what just happened wouldn't have. I need to be careful for my son, but I feel like I can trust you. Please don't let me down."

I kiss the top of her head, before running my hands through her sweaty hair. "I won't."

At least I hope I won't. I still haven't told her about Alec yet, but now isn't the time. Plus, I have no idea where to start.

"I should probably clean up and pick Alec up. It's my only day off this week and I promised him we'd do lots of fun activities." She runs her hands over my facial hair and smiles up at me. "I wish I could spend more time with you today, I really do, but you understand that I can't have you around my son right now, right? It's just too soon."

I smile and lean my forehead against hers. "Yeah. I wish we

could spend more time together too, but we have later tonight. I'll come see you after Alec is sleeping. Is that okay?"

"I'd love that." She wraps her arms around my neck, before gently pressing her lips against mine. "I'll text you once he falls asleep."

"I'll be waiting." I open the truck door and help her out to her feet, grabbing her face to kiss her, before she can walk away. "I'll be at the gym with my buddy Styx if you need me. Promise me that you'll call me if that asshole shows up again."

"Kash . . ."

"Promise me."

"I promise."

I kiss her one last time, before jumping back into my truck. "Good."

I have a feeling I'll be seeing him tonight no matter what . . .

chapter SEVENTEEN

KASH

BY THE TIME I MEET Styx at the gym, he's looking at me as if I've just lost my damn mind.

"What?" I question, while tossing my bag down by his desk. "Stop giving me that damn look."

Lifting a brow, he tosses a stack of folders into the top drawer and leans back in his seat. "Why does it look like you're ready to knock someone's head clear off their fucking shoulders?"

Growling to myself, I run my hands down my face and shake my head. "There's just an asshole I need to take care of later. Someone who's fucking with someone I care about and pissing me the hell off."

This has Styx straightening up, looking as if he's pissed off now. "Yeah . . ." He cracks his neck, while looking across the desk at me. I've realized that Styx and I are a lot alike. Protective and loyal as shit. "You need me to help out with this little prick?"

I smile and stand up. "Nah. Looks like he plans to come see me tonight. I'll handle him." I grip the top of the chair. "How's

Meadow? She miss seeing me dance yet?"

Styx laughs. "She's good. And not as much as you hope, fucker. She did tell me to tell you that you need to find a damn girl though so we can do some double dating bullshit."

I look up at him and can't help the smile that takes over. "Maybe I already found one."

"Fuuuck. You're gonna make my ass go on a double date." He smiles and stands up, pushing his chair in. "Meadow is gonna ride my ass now until we set one up. Might as well let your girl know."

"She's got a kid." My smile widens when I think about Alec. "A five-year-old son."

"You ready for that?" he asks, putting all joking aside. "I haven't seen you serious with anyone, brother. Think you can handle having two people not to let down?"

I nod my head. "Hell yeah, I'm ready. I *want* a family to take care of, man. Fuck being a stripper. The life gets lonely and does nothing for me but pass the time. It does nothing for my ass when I'm lying in bed at night, alone, with no one to hold and take care of. I want that special someone in my damn life. As soon as I get the rest of the money I need scraped up; I'm buying the warehouse I've been renting out and turning it into a training gym. I'm ready for serious shit to happen, Styx. No more stripping or fighting soon."

"That's some deep shit, brother." He grabs his keys from his desk, keeping his gaze on me. "Sounds like she might be good for you then. I've never heard you talk like this. I still remember when you told our asses to stay single for the job."

"Yeah, well I was a dumbass back then. Things have changed since I've been spending time with Alec."

"That's the kid your sister babysits, right?" he asks, before tilting back his bottle of water.

I nod my head and grip the top of the chair tighter, feeling stress and worry kick in. "Yeah . . . he's also Eden's son." I look up and flex my jaw. "She just doesn't know I've been spending time with him yet. It's too soon to tell her."

"Well fuck . . ." Styx looks as if he's worried for my ass. I am too, to be honest. "That's not good, man. That shit could blow up in your face and ruin your chances with this girl."

"I know that shit," I say stiffly. "I just need to find the right time to tell her. I'll figure it out."

"Let's hope so," he says. "Come on."

"Where we going?"

"You got the keys to the warehouse with you?"

I nod my head. "I always do."

"We both know there's no way you're making it through the day without letting off some steam." He waits for me to follow him out of his office, before locking it behind him. "Think you can take my ass?"

I stop in front of my truck and smile. "Are you serious?"

"Yup. Is that cool with you?"

"You don't train like I do so don't complain if I mess up your pretty face."

He smirks and straddles his motorcycle. "Reason for my woman to baby and take care of me. Ever dated a nurse before?"

"Nope."

"Then you don't know what it's like to be treated by a naked one. Don't worry about my fucking face."

With that he takes off, speeding out of the parking lot.

This motherfucker . . .

I jump into my truck and pull out a cigarette, lighting it.

I'm gonna need a couple of these before fighting my best friend. I should've known he'd do this shit for the simple fact he knows I need it right now.

Styx is standing by the door of the warehouse, waiting for me when I arrive a few minutes later.

He watches as I hop out of my truck and toss my cigarette down into the dirt. "Hurry up, asshole. I don't have all day."

I walk past him with a grin and unlock the door. "Don't be in such a hurry to get your ass kicked."

I hear him chuckle behind me as he follows me over to the makeshift ring. "How about we not waste time wrapping our fists and shit and get this over with."

"Seriously?" I turn to face him, watching him as he paces the ring.

"I've never wrapped my fists on the streets. I'm not about to start now just because we're in a ring." He smirks. "Let it out, motherfucker. Show me how pissed this asshole made you. Just don't forget I'm *not* him."

"Alright . . . you asked for it. But I'm warning you; you're not going to like it."

We circle each other around the ring a few times, stretching and cracking our bones, getting pumped up.

I can't believe I'm about to do this shit. I'll have to remember to make up for it later.

With a small smirk, I come at Styx swinging my left elbow at his jaw. It connects hard, sending him stumbling to the side.

He grins, keeping his eyes on me, making sure he has a good shot before swinging out and connecting his knee to my ribcage. The asshole is quicker than I expected.

"You get into a lot of fights as a kid or some shit?"

He flexes his chest and laughs. "More than I can count. So don't take it easy on me, asshole."

"Don't worry. I won't. Especially not now."

Coming at him, I wrap one arm around his neck and pull him to me, kneeing him in the stomach repeatedly, before releasing him and connecting my fist to his mouth.

He wants me to take this shit out on him. He wants to feel my rage right now. That's what he's going to get.

Spitting out blood, Styx stares me down, before growling out and swinging his fist to my right eye, causing me to lose my footing a little, before regaining composure.

"Who's this asshole?" he questions.

Just the thought of his name fires me up even more, causing me to swing out, connecting my fist to Styx's left side. "Knight fucking Stevens."

Styx pauses for a second. "Seriously? The fighter?" He catches me off guard, his elbow connecting to my chin.

"Yeah . . ."

"Why didn't you say that shit to begin with?"

"Because I hate to acknowledge the fact that he's known around here. That piece of shit already has a big head, thinking he can have whatever he wants. That shit stops now."

"Well shit . . ."

I turn around and grab the ropes, squeezing as tightly as I can. "He's never heard of me, but I'm going to make sure it's me he's fighting next week. He's going to feel my fucking wrath and learn that Eden is mine. Not his. I'll take care of her and *his* son. He's going to be hurting by the time I'm done with him. Trust me on that."

"I don't doubt it," Styx says from behind me. "Not one fucking bit. You really care about this Eden and her son. This is the real deal for you?"

I turn around to face Styx, letting him see the truth in my eyes. "I may have only known Eden for eight days, but yeah . . . what I feel inside is the real deal. The way she makes me feel when I'm around her; is the real fucking deal. I haven't wanted anything this bad in a long time, man. I'm gonna do whatever it takes to keep her and Alec in my life. I'm in too deep to walk away just because someone is threatening to fuck things up. Nah, I'm not going anywhere."

Knight is going to feel what it's like to lose everything he thinks he owns . . .

My entire body is covered with sweat, making it almost impossible to see because of it falling into my eyes with each thrust against the chair, I'm currently grinding against.

These leather pants are only making me that much hotter, reminding me that I need to get to the part of my routine where these fuckers come off.

Holding onto the top of the chair, I take my other hand and slowly run it down my chest and abs, before undoing my pants and lowering them down my hips a bit.

My head is so far away from where it should be right now that it's making it nearly impossible to get through this night; through this forced act with tons of women breathing down my body, trying their damned hardest to touch me.

To get a feel of my hard body beneath their fingertips. Just that one touch that will get them through the night once they get home to their beds.

I'm a dirty temptation for them to get off to.

I've been so far off my game tonight, my moves not really up to par to my usual nights, but surprisingly none of the women seem to notice.

They just keep grabbing at me with one hand, while tossing me money with their other.

I've been too distracted to really pay attention to any of them tonight; my mind staying on Eden and our earlier conversation about Knight and his threat.

I'm not gonna lie, I've scanned the crowd numerous times tonight looking for that son of a bitch to show up, just to come up empty.

Has me worrying that maybe he's decided to show back up at Eden's place instead, knowing that I'd be here, preoccupied by a bunch of women for a while.

It's been an hour since I've been able to get to my phone and my anxiety is at an all-time high, hoping like hell that I haven't missed a call or text from her, needing me there.

"Damn, take them offffff!"

"Yeeeeees! That's so hot! Work that chair for us, Kash!"

The yells from the crowd pull me back to the moment, reminding me that I need to get my shit together and make it through this song.

I have less than three minutes left on the stage and then I'm free to go. Shouldn't be that hard to handle, but somehow it is. Every song tonight has felt like ten minutes, dragging on.

Standing up, I kick the chair over and pull a random girl onto the stage, allowing her to remove my pants for me.

She takes this as an opportunity to touch my body, running her nails down my thighs and digging them in, seductively. I don't miss the fact that she also makes sure that at least three different parts of her body brush against my cock on her way to stand back up.

It's only slightly hard, but she bites her bottom lip and growls up at me anyway, obviously turned on.

Stepping out of my pants, I grab her hair and wrap it in my hand, before turning her around and bending her over.

I'm probably being a little rougher than usual right now, but fuck, I have a lot of anger built up right now.

Doesn't matter though, she only seems to like my roughness more, popping her ass out further for me to grind on it.

I only allow her the pleasure of feeling my cock against her for a few seconds, before I walk her off the stage and into the crowd where she belongs.

That's when I look up to see Eden lost in the crowd, her eyes locked on me and the girl who is still feeling up my body while she has the chance.

She knows this is only my job, but it's still hard to miss the slight disappointment and jealousy in her eyes.

Fuck, I hate that look.

Removing the girl's hands from my body, I push my way through the crowd, toward Eden.

She just stands there and watches as multiple women reach out to touch me as I walk past them, as if they have a right to feel me up. It's hard to make out the look on her face now, but she almost looks angry and embarrassed.

Her and I both know that as soon as I get to her that every set of eyes in this room will be focused on her and what I'm about to do.

But I don't give a shit. She's my girl and I want her and everyone here to know it.

I finally reach Eden and before she can say anything or walk away, I grab her face with both hands and kiss her so damn hard that she almost falls over, but reaches out to grab me instead.

Her lips feel so fucking good right now. *This* feels so fucking good; her in my arms; everyone here watching as I show her she's mine.

I needed this moment, especially with how much I've been worrying about Eden all night. Her being here has my heart fucking jumping with joy.

"Kash . . ." she says while fighting to catch her breath as she looks my face over. "What happened to your face?" She looks frightened for me as she runs her fingers over my bruises. "Did

Knight do this to you?"

I smile and shake my head. "Nah, this wasn't him, baby. Just a friend helping me release a little steam earlier."

Wanting her as close to me as possible, I slowly back her up against the wall, closing her in with my body. I lift both her hands above her head and run my lips up her neck, before kissing it. "So . . . Knight didn't show up here?"

"No," I whisper in her ear. "Remember this song?" I lift her up and wrap her legs around my waist, just like the first night we met. "I never did get to finish dancing to it for you."

There's less than a minute left of the song, but I begin grinding and dancing against her anyway, brushing my lips over hers.

Everything about this moment feels so much different than the first time. So damn intimate and personal as if there shouldn't be a crowd here to watch us.

She's completely relaxed this time, her body naturally moving with mine, our breathing heavy and needy as my hips move her up the wall with each slow thrust.

By the end of the song, her hands are digging into my shoulders, her legs squeezing me so tight that it almost hurts.

"Shit . . . I missed you today," I say against her lips. "A lot."

She smiles and moves her hands up to tangle in my hair. "Same here, Kash. I got here as soon as I could. Didn't want to wait until you got off."

I close my eyes and lower her legs down to the ground as she runs her fingertips over my face again. "I don't like seeing this. Does it hurt much?"

"No." I lean in and gently kiss her. It hurts, but I'm not gonna let her know just how much. "Can barely even feel it. Who's with Alec?"

"The babysitter. I asked her to come by for an hour as soon as he fell asleep. He exhausted himself today so I'm pretty sure he won't be waking up anytime soon."

I smile and run my hands through her hair. "Good. Still want me to come by when I get out of here?"

"I'd like that. I'll text you when I get home just to make sure he hasn't woken up."

We both look toward the stage when the next song blasts through the speakers, seeming louder than all the rest. "Fucking Colt and his hardcore rock. Scares the crowd every time it starts."

Eden laughs and stands up on her tippy toes to kiss me. "See you soon. And by the way . . . thanks for breakfast." She smiles, showing her appreciation.

With that she walks away, getting lost in the crowd.

I don't miss the fact that most the women stop watching the stage to look over at her and give her dirty looks.

Makes me want to protect her, but she just stands up straight and smiles, not letting them get to her.

I wait until she's outside and away from all the dirty looks before I rush over to the bar to get my phone from Sara.

She grins from ear to ear when she sees me. "Looks like you've found that special someone. Lucky her."

I grab my phone from her and can't help the smile that takes over. "Not as lucky as I am. Clock me out, will ya?"

"Sure thing, babe. Go get that beauty."

"I plan on it."

It takes me a bit to make my way through the crowd and to the locker room, but I quickly shower and get dressed, doing my best to hurry.

As soon as I'm pulling on a fresh pair of jeans, a text comes through from Eden letting me know it's okay to head over.

I smile like a fucking idiot in love. Something I've never done before. Especially over a simple text.

Shoving my phone into my hoodie and grabbing for my

keys, I walk out of the locker room, ready to get the hell out of here.

That's when I look up to see Knight sitting up at the bar, watching me with a cocky grin.

Keeping his gaze on me, he stands up and tilts back his glass, emptying it.

Then he winks and walks away, making his way toward the door with a confidence I don't like.

Fucking son of a bitch.

Letting my anger get the best of me, I fight my way through the herd of crazy women, not giving a shit that their hands are grabbing at every one of my body parts at the moment.

The only thing that matters is where that son of a bitch is going right now.

I don't like the look he gave me one bit. It was as if he was letting me know he won.

Once I finally make it to the door, I push past Kass and look around, not finding him anywhere.

"Fuuuck." I run my hands through my wet hair and turn back to face Kass, about to lose my shit. "Where did he go?" I growl.

"If you're looking for the same asshole from before, he jumped into the passenger side of some car and sped out of here."

"Thanks, brother." I slap his chest, before rushing over to my truck and speeding out of here my damn self.

I honestly have no idea what I'll end up doing if that prick is parked outside Eden's, but I know one thing . . .

I'll kill him if he puts his hands on her again . . .

chapter EIGHTEEN

Eden

I STAND IN THE DOORWAY of Alec's room, watching him as he sleeps, looking so peaceful and comfortable.

Hannah said he didn't wake up once when I was gone and that's what I was hoping for.

The idea of him waking to me not being here makes me feel sick to my stomach.

I struggled a while with my decision to leave and check on Kash tonight, but honestly, I *needed* to see that he was okay.

After the promise Knight made, I was almost positive he'd show up like he said and cause trouble for Kash.

I never planned on being gone for longer than I had to and when I called Hannah and told her my plan was to stop by the club to see someone, she sounded more than happy to stop by for a bit.

Even though I should be happy that Knight didn't show up at the club tonight, I can't help but to worry still. Knight's an asshole. He'll still do what he said. He always does.

When I hear a vehicle pull up outside, I softly close Alec's door, careful not to wake him, before walking into the living room and looking out the window.

A little black sports car is sitting across the street, so I'm assuming it must be for one of the neighbors.

It hasn't been long since I texted Kash, so I suppose it's a little too soon for him to be outside.

A few minutes later I hear another vehicle pull up, so I look out the window again, hoping it's Kash.

My heart speeds up with excitement at the sight of his truck parked out front.

With a huge smile, I unlock the door and open it, watching as he jumps out of his truck and walks up the sidewalk.

His face looks even more bruised up and swollen when he steps into the porchlight. The darkness of the club hid them better.

"Hi," he says with a small smirk.

"Hi back." I smile and step out of the way, allowing him to come inside. "Just be quiet."

As soon as I close the door, I feel Kash come up behind me, his hard body pressing firmly against me. "I'll do my best."

I close my eyes and swallow, when I feel Kash's hands move down my body and grab my hips. "Your hands . . ."

He kisses my neck, before moving around to whisper in my ear. "What about them?"

"They feel so good." I barely get the words out, because he begins kissing his way around to the front of my neck. "And your lips . . . shit, Kash."

He spins me around and cups my face with both hands, brushing his thumbs over my lips. "Want me to stop?"

I shake my head and wrap my arms around his neck. "No," I whisper. "But we have to be careful. I can't have . . . sex. Not with

Alec in the next room."

He smiles against my lips. "I'm not here to have sex with you, Eden. I'm here to spend time with you." He grabs my hand. "Come on."

He guides me over to the couch, pulling me into his lap. Then he reaches for the blanket on the back of the couch and covers us up. "I like this," I admit, while snuggling into the warmth of his strong body. "What now?"

He reaches for the remote and places it in my hand. "Pick out a movie." He kisses my neck, before smiling against it. "Now we relax as I massage you. The clean version. You know . . . since I'm not naked and all."

Chills run over my body as he pulls me against him and begins rubbing my shoulders and arms as I search through movies to watch.

I could seriously get used to this and it's easy to picture the three of us hanging out, watching movies and spending time together. Something Knight was never into.

"This looks good."

"I'm good with whatever," he says into my hair. "Whatever makes you happy."

I smile and kiss his arm. "It's working . . ."

"What's working?"

"You getting me used to you," I admit. "But I like it."

"How much?"

"A lot more than I ever expected."

He wraps his arms tighter around me, making sure I'm comfortable as the movie starts. "Good. That's what I wanted."

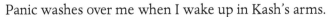

Panic washes over me when I wake up in Kash's arms.

We were both so comfortable on the couch that we fell

asleep, during the movie.

"Kash," I whisper yell. "Wake up. We fell asleep!"

I feel Kash move beneath me, before he sits up and presses his lips against my neck. "Shit. I'm sorry. What time is it?"

I look up at the clock to see it's just past six.

Luckily Alec never wakes up this early so I begin to calm down a bit and think rationally.

"Don't apologize. I fell asleep too." I remove the blanket from Kash and straddle his lap, pressing a quick kiss to his lips. "He didn't wake up or else he'd still be in here sleeping on the floor next to us. He always does that if he wakes up to me sleeping on the couch. So we're good for a few minutes. Long enough to say bye at least."

Kash smiles and it instantly melts my heart. It's so beautiful and sincere. "I'm glad I get to see you before work at least."

"Me too . . ." I lean in and press my forehead against his. "I have a feeling work won't be so bad now."

With a small growl, he grabs my hips and pushes me further down into him. His morning erection has me letting out a small moan as it grinds into me. "Work might be hell for me now. Fuck, Eden." He brushes my hair away from my neck, before kissing it. "I'm gonna need to relieve myself in the shower."

I smile when he does, knowing something smartass is most likely coming next. "But I'll be sure to think about you as I'm stroking it slow and hard."

I laugh and slap his chest. "Now I'll be picturing that in my head all day at work, while I'm rubbing down dirty, sweaty men."

He moans and sets me to my feet. "Good."

"Not good!" I stand to my tippy toes and wrap my arms around his neck when he stands. "How am I supposed to focus on work when I'm turned on and thinking about you?"

"How about this . . ." he lifts a brow. "I'll try to come visit you. Maybe give you that massage I owe you."

"I could like that . . . maybe."

"Mommy!"

"Shiiiit. You've gotta go, Kash." I push my way out of Kash's arms and rush over to the hallway to poke my head around the corner. "I'll be there in a minute, baby. Just stay there! Don't get out of bed yet."

When I turn back to face Kash, he's got his hood pulled over his head and he's standing by the door with it open and ready for him to make a quick escape. "I'll see you later," he mouths. "Take care of the little guy."

I cover my face, embarrassed that I'm rushing him out like this. Like I'm some kind of teenager. "Thank you," I mouth back. "Bye."

He blows me a kiss that melts my damn world, before walking outside and gently closing the door behind him.

"Holy shit," I breathe out.

I stand here for a few seconds with my hand over my racing heart, before I make my way to Alec's bedroom.

"Hey, baby boy."

He smiles up at me and stretches. "Hey mommy. Is it time to go to Hannah's yet?"

I shake my head and walk over to kiss him on the forehead. "Not quite yet, baby. It's a little early. Why don't you lay back down while mommy takes a shower and gets ready for work, okay."

He yawns and lays back down. "Okay, I'll do that. I'll lay back down and close my eyes. Can you let me know when it's time, mommy?"

I smile at how sweet my little boy is. This kid truly lights up my life and getting to see Kash this morning on top of it, only makes it feel like today is going to be a good day. I really need one too.

"Sure, baby boy." I rub my hand through his messy hair. "Be back soon."

When we pull up at Hannah's, she's waiting outside like usual, but this time she's smiling at me as if she knows something I don't.

She waits until I say goodbye to Alec, before turning to me and finally speaking. "So . . . who were you going to see at the club last night? I was too tired to ask before I took off."

My face turns red as I realize I'm about to admit I'm sort of dating one of the strippers. "His name is Kash and that's all I'm saying right now."

Her eyes grow wide and her mouth drops open in surprise. "Whoa."

"What?"

She shakes her head. "Nothing. Cool name, that's all." She lets out a small laugh. "You're going to be late again."

I look down at my watch to see that she's right. "Shit. Gotta go!

"You really need to set your watch like ten minutes ahead. I swear!" She yells to me as I rush to my jeep.

"Good idea! Thanks again. I don't know what I'd do without you."

"No problem." She smiles and waves me off before disappearing inside.

I spent a little too much time in the shower this morning, apparently.

Guess I have Kash to thank for that . . .

KASH

SHIT . . .

When I heard Alec's tired little voice this morning calling for Eden from his bedroom, I wanted nothing more than for him to come out and see me standing there in his house.

I wanted to see the excitement in his eyes that's always there whenever he sees me show up at my sister's house for him.

It fucking hurt that I couldn't let him know I was there. I threw on my hood as if that would somehow stop him from noticing me if he were to walk into the living room.

Truthfully, I knew Alec would know it was me no matter what. The kid has been around me far too many times to not notice this old hoodie I wear.

But I did it for Eden's sake. I knew how much it would hurt her if she found out that way. Alec rushing over to me, calling me Hunter would fuck with Eden's head, making her lose all trust for me.

That's the last thing I want to happen. I know now more

than ever that I need to have that talk with Eden and soon. If I'm not the one to tell her, it can ruin everything we've built over the last nine days.

The thought causes my chest to ache.

I care about Eden more than I've ever cared about a woman before. Some may say I'm an idiot for falling so quickly, but sometimes the fall happens so damn fast that you don't even know until you've already fallen.

And after falling asleep with Eden in my arms last night, getting to feel how fucking good it was to have her let go around me and allow her walls to come down; I know without a doubt that I'll never get over that feeling for as long as I live.

The way her small body melted into my arms, tangled up in me as if I was her safe haven had my heart beating, making me feel more alive than ever. I want that feeling every damn day.

I want to be her safety; the one she can come to when she needs comfort and protection from everything bad in this fucked up world.

I want to be that for her and Alec.

That's exactly why I set up dinner plans for tomorrow with Styx and Meadow. I want her to see what it's like to be a part of my life. I want to know what that feels like before I break the truth to her and possibly push her away.

I'm a selfish asshole for not telling her in the first place. I know that and I hate myself for it.

But when it comes to a woman like Eden, you do stupid things sometimes in fear of losing something that was probably too good for you to hold onto in the first place.

"Fuuuuck!" I run my hands through my sweaty hair and step out of my truck.

That's when I notice the same black car that was parked in front of Eden's house last night, now parked across the street.

Keeping my gaze on the sports car, I pull out a cigarette and lean against my truck, letting it known that I see them.

It's not until I'm half-way through my cigarette that the car finally pulls out of the parking lot across the street and slowly drives past me, giving me a clear view of Knight in the passenger seat.

He flexes his jaw, staring me up and down, making it pretty fucking aware that he's sizing me up.

I take one last drag off my cigarette and smirk, before flicking it toward the street, letting him know he doesn't intimidate me.

Like I told Eden; I'm not going anywhere.

He wants a fight and that's exactly what he's getting in six days. I just have one more fight to get me to that spot.

This shit is happening when we're both prepared and ready to go head to head. He just doesn't know it yet.

Pushing my hood back, I give the little car one last look before heading toward the door. From what Riley told me before, Knight isn't allowed here anymore, due to him making a huge scene once when Eden was working.

Riley had to push him out the door and make it clear he's not to step foot into the parlor again.

Good to know the son of a bitch is staying off the property at least. He's already fucking with the woman I care about. He fucks with family and he's for sure dead.

Riley immediately looks up from the computer and gives me a surprised look when I step inside. "What happened to your face?"

I shrug and walk up to the counter. "I don't know what you're talking about?" I smile when she does. "Styx happened to my face. Him being a good friend and all."

"Alriiiight."

I grab her head and kiss it, before rushing past her and down the hall.

"She has a client in ten minutes, Kash!"

"Good to know!" I yell back.

I catch her shaking her head, right before I reach Eden's room and push the door open.

Before Eden can manage to say anything about me showing up unannounced, I stalk inside and pick her up, setting her on top of the table.

With a small growl, I wrap my hand into the back of her hair and press my lips against hers, kissing her hard and deep.

My heart flutters in my chest the moment her tongue swirls around mine and she moans into my mouth.

Fuck, this woman does things to me I can't explain.

"Kash," she breathes against my lips. "I have a client soon."

I smile against her lips and run my thumbs over her cheekbones. "I know . . ." I press my body further into hers, making my erection known. "Cancel it."

She digs her nails into my arms and closes her eyes, most likely fighting her need for me to take her. "I wish it was that easy, Kash."

Pushing her further onto the table, I climb above her and settle my body between her legs. I slowly run my hands up her sides, before reaching up to grab her throat.

I see the excitement in her eyes at the idea of me being rough with her and I love it. She's no longer holding back with me.

Keeping my hand on her throat, I grind my body into hers and lean in to bite her bottom lip. "Are you sure it's too late to cancel? Fuuuuck me, Eden. I want to rip your clothes off and fuck you against the wall."

She lets out another little moan, enjoying the feel of me

between her legs, before she finally slaps my chest and smiles. "Dammit, Kash. You're good. Really damn good, but my client is most likely checking in right now. I can't cancel with her right in the lobby."

I growl against her lips, before kissing her one last time and stepping down off the table. "I want to do something with you tomorrow. Can I have you for a few hours?"

She smiles as I help her back down to her feet. "Depends . . . what do you want me for?"

I grab her waist and pull her against me, wanting to feel her close to me for as long as possible, before I have to leave her until tomorrow. "Styx hates double dates and his woman wants us all to go on one. Help me annoy him and then spend a little alone time with me after. You in?"

"Styx . . ." she kisses my face. "The one that messed up this handsome face of yours?"

I nod. "Yup."

"I think I'm up for annoying him." She smiles against my lips. "I'll have my father come by for a few hours. Alec's been wanting to show him his new room set up."

"Perfect." I cup her face and kiss her, causing her to moan against my lips and wrap her arms around my neck.

"Kash . . . you should . . ." I kiss her again, making it hard for her to get her words out. "Dammit . . . you're making this hard."

Smirking, I grab her hand and lower it down my body and down to my hard cock. "Like this?"

She nods her head and rubs me through my pants, her breathing picking up. "Mmmhmmm . . . exactly like this."

Locking eyes with hers, I back her against the wall and pick her up, wrapping her legs around my waist.

"Maybe it's not too late," she breathes. "Maybe they're not here yet . . ."

I'm just about to reach over and lock the door, when someone knocks on it, scaring the shit out of Eden.

She jumps out of my arms and quickly fixes herself, fighting to catch her breath. "Shit . . . Shit . . ."

I push down on my erection and growl under my breath, sexually frustrated. "Fuck. Looks like they're here."

We both smile as she fixes her hair and splashes a little water on her face to cool off.

"I'll text you later with a time for tomorrow." I grab the back of her head and kiss her one last time, hating the fact that I have to leave her now.

"I so hate you right now," she says against my lips.

"But you'll love me later . . ."

I open the door and smile when some pretty brunette looks me up and down and then shoots her attention over to Eden who is still looking hot and bothered.

"Very nice . . . talk about being lucky."

I can practically feel her eyes burning into my backside as I walk down the hall.

Riley immediately laughs when she notices the look of disappointment on my face. "Sorry. I held her off for as long as I could. She's really damn annoying so I had to let her go."

"Thanks," I say sarcastically. "Still love you though."

"Love you too, punk." She stands up and fixes my hair. "When is your next fight before the big one?"

"Tomorrow night."

She pushes my shoulder. "Good luck, babe."

"I won't need it." I grin and walk outside, looking to see if Knight is anywhere around.

The asshole's lucky he's not . . .

chapter TWENTY

Eden

KASH LEFT ME HOT AND bothered last night at work, making it nearly impossible to get through my clients without thinking about all the dirty ways he could fuck me against the wall.

The way his hard body moved between my legs was so damn hot that it had me sweating every time I thought about it. I swear I even almost passed out at one point from the heat the memory brought.

I can't even count the number of times my clients had to ask me if I was alright before the night was over.

It really makes me believe he did it on purpose just to leave me thinking about him all night. He knew it would only make me crave him more and he was right.

The thought leaves me smiling as I pull out of the driveway and head toward the park. The same one Kash and I played baseball at last week. The same one we *almost* had sex at.

I also think he asked me to meet him there on purpose as well. He and I both know exactly how hot that night was and going there again is only going to bring up memories and leave me on edge with need tonight.

As soon as I told him it wasn't a good idea for him to pick me up at the house, he suggested we meet here.

I swear I could hear the smile in his voice as he spoke, setting the plans in motion.

He wants to play . . . so I'll play.

We'll just see who gives in first before the night is over.

I asked my father to stay over for a few hours, giving me enough time for dinner and whatever else Kash has planned for after.

As expected he was fine with it and happy to see me out doing something for myself for once. The only thing I feel guilty about is lying to Alec and telling him I was going out with a few friends.

I plan to talk to Alec about Kash soon, but I just don't know how to bring him up. I mean do I call him my guy friend? Or do I just come out and say that mommy has a new boyfriend?

I've never had to do this before and it's not easy. It's really damn hard. He may be only five but he understands that his daddy and I used to love each other very much and that's why he was born. I have no idea how he's going to feel finding out that I'm letting another man into our lives that isn't Knight.

Alec doesn't open up easily and let people in. It scares me that he might not give Kash a chance, but scares me even more that he will and things won't work out in the long run. I don't want to add any stress or heartache to my son's life, when he's already had so much over the years, due to Knight so easily abandoning him.

He's been scarred enough by a man that's supposed to be there for him.

But I feel like Kash is different. He makes me believe he's

different and I want nothing more than to believe that with all my heart.

I just need more time before I make such a huge, lifechanging decision. I've only known Kash for ten days. It shocks me that I'm even thinking about this so soon, but everything with Kash seems to be different.

I plan to talk to Kash about that tonight and let him know that I'm just not quite ready for them to meet yet, but soon. Maybe another week or so. I don't know for sure but I have a feeling that I'll know when the time is right. Or maybe it already is and I'm just too scared to see it.

Kash is already parked over by the baseball field, waiting on me, in the same spot he parked the last time.

He immediately smiles and jogs over to my jeep, opening the door for me. I can't deny how his gorgeous smile has my heart aching in the best way possible.

Without saying anything, he grabs my waist and pulls me into his arms, pressing his lips against mine with a desperation that has my heart going crazy for him.

He makes me feel needed and wanted, a feeling I'm afraid of losing. I hate being afraid, but with Kash it's a good kind of scared that's completely worth it.

We're both breathing heavily, with my arms wrapped around his neck when he pulls away to look me in the eyes. "Fuck, I've been wanting to do that all damn day." He tangles his hands into the back of my hair and kisses me again, this time much harder and deeper, making it almost impossible to catch my breath.

"Oh yeah . . ." Smiling, I reach in between us and rub my hand over his erection, before running my tongue over his ear. "I've been wanting to do *this* all day. Too bad your friends are waiting for us to have dinner."

Kash places his hand over mine and lets out a sexy little

growl that has my pussy aching for him. "You trying to get me back for yesterday, baby?" He lets go of my hand and reaches around to cup my ass, practically lifting me up off the ground. "I'll fuck you on the dinner table if it comes down to it, baby. Don't test me. The whole restaurant can watch."

I feel him smile against my neck, before he bites it and backs me into his truck. Keeping his body against mine, he reaches for the door and opens it. "You ready?"

I swallow, still trying to compose myself from his words. "I'm a little nervous, but ready."

He pulls me further into his arms and tilts my chin up, until our eyes meet. "You're *my* girl. No need to be nervous, ever. Got it?"

I nod my head and smile. Hearing him call me *his* girl has my heart doing crazy things.

"Good." With that he boosts me up into the truck and shuts the door, before walking over to the other side and getting in himself.

I wait until he takes off, before leaning over and grabbing his thigh. That's when I notice a black and pink baseball mitt in the backseat.

He must notice me looking, because he smirks. "Hope you're up for a little ball after dinner. We have a game to finish."

I laugh and squeeze his thigh. "Is that right? Are we playing with or without clothes this time?"

"We'll definitely start out with clothes." He grabs my hand and places it on his dick, causing chills of excitement to run all throughout my body. It's so damn hot when he's in control. "I just can't promise we'll end with clothes. Besides . . . he nods down at his crotch. I'm pretty sure you want me naked. I don't blame you."

There he goes again turning me on and making me laugh

at the same time. "So does that mean it'll just be the two of us playing ball? Or is there going to be four grown adults running around in their underwear like lunatics? Should I be worried? Is that part of the whole double dating scene."

A small smile creeps up on his lips. "Definitely just the two of us." He reaches for my hand and holds it now. "It'll always just be the two of us . . . until it's the three of us."

My heart practically jumps out of my chest from his words.

Why does the idea of that make me feel both happy and scared?

I think I know though. I don't want to lose Kash, that's why. Because deep down inside I want it to be that way too. The three of us . . .

We sit in silence, my hand still in his, for the rest of the way to the restaurant.

But I can tell by the way he keeps glancing over at me with that little smile of his that he knows his words affected me in a good way.

He's just giving me this moment to prepare before meeting his friends.

"Styx and Meadow are inside already. They saved us a table so there wouldn't be a wait." He shifts the truck into park and reaches over to grab my chin. "They're like family to me. Just be yourself and I promise everything else will just fall into place and they'll fall for you just as I did."

With a small smile, I grab the back of his hair and lean in to press my lips against his. I love how he can manage to make me feel so comfortable with his words. He always seems to know the right things to say. "I'm ready."

KASH

Just knowing that Eden is less than ten seconds away from meeting two of my best friends has me smiling so damn big that I can hardly contain it.

The thing about us boys is that we never bring a girl to meet up with our *Walk of Shame* family until we know she's the one we want to be serious with. In all the years I have known them, Eden is the first one I've invited out with us.

Fuck if that doesn't mean something big to me.

Grabbing onto her hand, I pull her against me, keeping her close as I pull the door to the restaurant open and guide her inside.

My eyes immediately seek out Styx and Meadow sitting to the far left, kissing and flirting as if they're the only two in the damn place.

"That's them." I point over to their table. "Think they'll even notice we showed up for dinner? Or should we just leave now and go play some ball?" I wink, causing her to wrap her arm around my neck and kiss my nose.

"I don't know . . . I guess we'll see. If they don't notice us within the first two minutes then we'll leave and have our own fun."

Her response has me laughing, which has Meadow looking over and waving for us as if we don't notice the two practically fucking on the table.

"Too late now," I mutter. "Story of my life lately. My timing is has been really shitty."

Grabbing Eden's waist, I kiss her on the cheek, before guiding her over to the table, where Styx and Meadow are both standing up now.

"Oh thank goodness." Meadow reaches for Eden's hand and

pulls her in for a hug, talking next to her ear. "My date's been working on getting me to *bed* since the moment we walked in the door. Not sure how much longer I could've held him off."

"I have all night, baby. Don't think for one fucking second that I'm going to be tired anytime soon. I have a lot of stamina. Don't you forget it," Styx says with a cocky grin, before looking back at Eden. "Sorry, babe. You'll get used to us."

I wait until Meadow releases her hold on Eden, before I pull her into my arms and whisper against her ear. "You sure you don't want to just escape now? Last chance."

Eden places her hand on my abs and grins. "Nope! A little too late for that." She looks Styx's bruised face over as I pull out a chair for her to sit down. "And I thought his face was a hot mess. You boys really did a number on each other."

I laugh and take my seat next to her, watching as Meadow smiles across the table at Eden.

"Oh this one loves it. A good excuse to keep me being his nurse long after hours. He may look tough but he looks for any excuse to have me make him *feel better.*"

Styx grins and nods his head at me. "Told you, brother. All good."

Everyone talks and laughs easily for the next hour as if Eden has known Styx and Meadow for just as long as I have.

Shit, that makes me so damn happy. I love seeing how easily they accept her and she accepts them.

"Oh wow." Meadow's eyes widen as she laughs. "He sounds like a fun kid that keeps you on your toes."

"He's a hyper little guy. Definitely keeps me busy, but I wouldn't have it any other way. He's the best thing to ever happen to me." Eden smiles and leans across the table a bit. "What about you and Styx? Any plans for a kid anytime soon?"

I catch a look in Styx's eyes that tells me maybe he's been

thinking about it. Truth is, I could definitely see him having a family with Meadow.

Meadow smiles, before taking a drink of her water. "I don't know. Haven't really talked about it. We'll give it a little more time. I don't think either of us is in a rush."

"It's definitely better to wait when you know for a fact you're both ready. That's something I didn't do."

Growing impatient with the women chatting, while Styx gives me grumpy looks for getting him into this double date, I grab Eden's chair, pulling it closer to me as she continues her conversation with Meadow.

It's when I press my lips against her neck, that she pauses mid-sentence and closes her eyes.

Styx takes this opportunity of distraction to get to Meadow too, because when I look over, Styx is pulling Meadow into his lap, whispering things into her ear.

"I love my friends. I do . . ." I brush Eden's hair away from her neck, before kissing it again, making my way up to her ear. "But I only get you for a little while longer. Let's get out of here, babe."

Surprising her, I stand up, lifting her up with me, not giving a crap that everyone in the restaurant is watching us. "Kash!" She laughs and grabs onto my back as I lift her higher, so her feet are off the ground.

"Love you both. Let's do this again." I reach into my pocket and throw a pile of money onto the table, not giving a shit how much it is. "Dinner's on me."

"I'll get your number from Kash," Meadow says from Styx's lap as Eden attempts to look back at her. "I'm pretty sure we're out of here too."

Styx growls before biting her bottom lip and grinding beneath her. "We're definitely out of here, babe."

"Sounds good. It was . . ." I don't even give Eden the chance to finish saying bye, before I'm rushing through the restaurant and setting her down in front of my truck, desperate to get out of here and get her alone. "I didn't even get to say bye."

"My friends love you. You can say bye next time. It's dark. Perfect time to play ball." I wink and open the truck door for her, boosting her ass up and slapping it. "Let's go."

Excitement courses through me as memories of the first time we attempted to play baseball take over, causing my cock to grow hard.

Shit . . . I hope we get to finish this time . . .

chapter
TWENTY-ONE

Eden

WE PULL UP AT THE park and my heart immediately begins racing with excitement when I realize we're the only ones here.

I'm not gonna lie, the thought of Kash slamming me against the fence and fucking me right here in the open has my whole body on fire.

If it weren't for the teenagers that showed up last time and interrupted us, I would've let him take me anyway he wanted.

That's how excited he gets me and I've never felt this adventurous when it comes to sex. Knight always tried to get me to let him have sex with me in bathrooms at bars or in his training room before fights, but I never wanted to.

All I kept thinking about was someone possibly catching us and Knight getting a big head and gloating about it to his friends.

But with Kash . . . the thought of him taking me anywhere he wants—even here at a baseball field—is extremely exciting.

"You thinking about me over there?" Kash undoes my seat-belt and reaches in the back for his equipment, handing me the black and pink mitt. "If you're trying to think of ways to get me naked, all you have to do it turn on some music. That usually does the trick."

"Is that all it takes? So when you meet my dad I should make sure there's no music?" I grin and jump out of the truck, shutting the door behind me.

I can't believe I just mentioned him meeting my father, but it came out so naturally as if it's inevitable for it to happen at some point.

A few seconds later, Kash slips in behind me, wrapping his arms around my waist. "So you like me enough to keep my clothes on . . . fuck, talk about making me one happy guy." He kisses my neck and squeezes me tighter. "I like the idea of meeting your family. But we'll see how you feel *after* I beat you at ball."

With that he laughs and bends down to pick up his equipment, before jogging over to the fence.

I stand here for a few seconds and watch as he strips his shirt off and picks up the bat, flashing me the sexiest smile I've ever seen.

"Any day now," he teases. "Should we start out where we left off or start a new game?"

"Hmmm. Maybe a fresh one." I grab the bat out of his hand and give him a cocky grin. "Well pitcher . . . any day now."

He lifts a brow and begins backing up as if me teasing him only has him pumped up more and ready to go.

"I think we need to change the rules a bit." He says once he reaches the pitcher's mound.

"Okay." I position my hands on the bat and flash him a smile. "Tell me these new rules and maybe I'll agree on them."

"If you miss this ball." He tosses it up and catches it with confidence. "Then I get to kiss you . . ." he lowers his eyes toward my pussy. "Right there."

I can practically feel my face turn red as I imagine him between my legs, tasting me. "And what if I hit it?"

"Then I'll take you on another date." He smirks and gets into position, looking so damn sexy.

"I can agree to those new rules, Mr. Cocky."

He does this little thing to make me believe he's about to pitch the ball, but then stops and changes positions.

"What are you doing over there? Come on!" I yell out.

He cracks his neck and smiles. "Making sure you miss this ball. That's what."

Right when I lower the bat and laugh, he pitches the ball. Excitement and adrenaline courses through me as I quickly swing the bat out, my heart racing with anticipation.

Kash smiles when the crack of the bat hitting the ball rings out through the park.

He runs over and stops in front of me. "I was secretly hoping you'd hit it." He wraps his fist into the back of my hair and leans down to whisper in my ear. "I can always kiss you down there after the date."

I swallow and reach for the extra ball he brought. Keeping a smile on my face, I walk over to the pitcher's mound and run my fingers over the dirt on the ball. "If you miss this ball, then you have to cook me dinner."

"And if I hit it?" he raises the bat and swings out as if he knows there's no way he's missing it.

"Then you get to give me that massage you promised. And I'll let you do it in the nude so you can do it to your full ability."

He bites his bottom lip as if he's picturing it now. "I so fucking agree to these rules."

Putting on a serious face, I pitch the ball and watch as it flies across the park, Kash hitting it further than the last time we were here.

Shaking my head, I walk toward him and stop in front of him. Feeling his breath against my neck as he moves his body up against mine has me wanting him like crazy right now.

I grin and reach for the top of his jeans. "I changed my mind . . . I say we start out where we left off now. This game didn't count."

With a small smirk, he grabs my waist and slowly backs me against the fence. "That would be with you pinned against this fence with me about to *fuck* you so good that you'll forget any other guys exist."

"Oh yeah?" I whisper, while unbuttoning his jeans. "I definitely want to start there, Kash."

He flexes his jaw and grabs onto the fence, watching me as I lower his jeans. "You sure that's where you want to start? I've been craving to be inside you for days. It's not going to be gentle or sweet."

Wanting nothing more than for him to take me how he wants, I run my hands up his chest, before wrapping my arms around his neck. "I don't want you gentle or sweet. I want you just the way you are."

With a small growl, he pins me against the fence with his body. "Fuuuck. I hope no one interrupts us, because this time I'm not stopping."

Putting all gentleness aside, Kash bites the top of my tank top before ripping it open with his hands. Goosebumps cover my entire body as I grip onto the fence behind me and hold on as he yanks my jeans and panties down my legs.

With this look of need in his eyes I've never seen before, he bites my bottom lip and grabs my ass, lifting me up so that my legs are wrapped around his waist, just like the last time he had me pinned against this fence.

I moan into his mouth and dig my nails into his shoulders

when I feel him slam into me, stopping once we fills me completely.

"I need you to tell me something," he breathes against my lips. "And I need you to mean it."

"What?" I dig my fingers deeper into his shoulders and squeeze him with my legs when he begins pumping in and out of me. "Holy . . . Kash . . . that feels . . . good . . . so damn good."

He pushes deeper inside and stops, leaning in so our mouths are brushing together. "Tell me I'm the only one you want inside of you. That there'll be no one else fucking you the way I do."

The truth is, I can't even imagine another man being inside me the way Kash is right now and feeling as good as it does. I don't want any other men. I want him. So fucking much.

"There'll be only you, Kash. I don't want anyone else. I mean it."

"Good. That's all I needed to hear."

Slamming his lips against mine, he pushes me up the fence with one hard thrust, causing me to grab onto his hair for support.

With each perfect move of his hips, excitement and need overwhelm me, causing a mix of chills and heat to run throughout my entire body.

I close my eyes and lean my head against the fence when Kash's hand moves up to brush over my throat. "It's okay," I breathe. "Don't be scared of hurting me."

"Fuck!" He growls and grabs my throat, gently squeezing it as he continues to thrust in and out of me, his thick dick slamming into me hard and deep.

I open my eyes and look around, a new kind of excitement filling me as I take in the open field around us.

Anyone could show up at any moment and all Kash is thinking about is me and his need to take me.

I find it extremely hot.

My body tenses around his and I moan out the moment I feel his thumb reach in between us to rub my clit.

"Oh fuuuckkk . . ." I reach behind me and hold onto the fence, breathing heavily as he continues to fuck me and rub me at the same time. "Keep going," I beg. "I'm so close."

He rubs his mouth up my neck, before biting it and thrusting into me at the same time, causing me to clamp around his dick and scream out in pleasure as an orgasm rushes through me.

I can feel him smile against me, before he moves around to kiss my lips. "Hold on for this part. Okay, baby."

I nod my head and hold onto the fence as tightly as I can.

He grabs my waist with both hands, his fingers digging in as he pounds into me hard and fast.

So hard and fast that I feel as if I'm close to another orgasm.

Holy shit . . . this feels so damn good. I can't imagine anyone fucking as good as Kash.

He thrusts into me a few more times, before pushing in as deep as he can and growling against my lips as he comes.

Him filling me has another orgasm washing through me, causing me to moan against his mouth and wrap my arms around his neck for support.

As soon as I'm able to catch my breath, Kash kisses me, being gentle and careful as if he wants to take care of me now.

He holds me against the fence for a few minutes, our lips touching as we fight to catch our breath, before he lowers me to the ground.

"You okay?" he questions, while caressing my cheek.

I smile and nod my head. "More than okay, Kash. I told you not to be gentle and I meant it."

He smiles back and helps me get cleaned up, before slipping his shirt over my head and getting dressed himself. "Sorry about the shirt. I'll replace it."

I shake my head and walk into his arms as he holds them out for me. "This one will do just fine."

He kisses the top of my head and smiles against it. "Then it's yours." He grabs my hand and walks out into the open field, before laying down and pulling me into his arms. "We have a little more time before I have something to take care of tonight. Something important to help me open my training gym. My dad used to train fighters and I always thought we'd open a gym together."

I lay my head on his chest and look up at the stars, wishing that we could stay out here like this all night. Us just talking. "Where's your father now?" I hate to ask this. Worry kicks in that I might get an answer I don't want.

"He passed away three years ago." He holds me tighter. "I'm doing this gym all on my own."

"I'm sorry, Kash. So sorry to hear that." I kiss his arm, wanting to show him I care. "What happens after you open this gym? Will you be working at the club too?"

"Nope. I'm done with the club as soon as I get the cash I need. It's the only reason I really started stripping in the first place." Kash grabs my hand and places it on his chest, holding it over his racing heart. "It feels really nice being here with you, Eden. I know you don't want to rush into anything and I don't blame you. It's not just yourself you have to worry about. But I want you to know I care about you a lot. It's not often that I let women into my life. You're the first since high school."

My heart swells up from Kash's words and I find myself smiling so big that it hurts. First I find out that he won't be staying at the club much longer and now this. I wasn't expecting either. "I care about you, too. You have no idea how much it means to me that you understand my situation and respect it. It's just that . . . well Alec is still so young. I don't want to confuse him if I don't have to. I need to know one hundred percent that you're in it for the long run before I even think about you two meeting. You understand, right?"

He nods his head and smiles, but I can see the worry in his eyes as if he has something he wants to tell me. "I'm in it for as long as you'll have me, Eden. I'm not going anywhere. I meant what I said. But I know it's still early. I need you to trust me. When the times comes . . . I have something important to tell you. Promise me you'll let me tell you when you know the time is right."

"I promise, Kash. If that's what you want." I relax into him and close my eyes, getting comfortable as he begins rubbing my head.

We lay this way for close to an hour before I feel my phone go off in my pocket.

It's getting late so I know it's Alec, calling me before he's about ready to fall asleep.

"I've gotta go," I whisper. "I want to be home before Alec goes to bed."

He stands up and helps me to my feet. "I love that about you."

I wrap my arms around his waist and just hold him for a few minutes, not wanting to leave him yet. It only seems to get harder the more we spend time together.

Looking down at me, he grabs my face and kisses me. "Call me when you get off work tomorrow?"

I nod my head and jump inside my jeep when Kash opens the door for me. "I can do that. "I smile and grab his neck, pulling him down so I can kiss him one last time. "Goodnight."

He smiles and shuts the door, before jogging over to his truck and jumping inside.

I get this sinking feeling in my stomach as I drive off, leaving Kash in the parking lot. I hate the feeling of leaving him.

Maybe it's about time I talk to Alec about him. It's too late tonight and I need a little time to clear my head and think it over before I figure out how to explain Kash to him.

I hope tomorrow is the right time and I'm not being stupid by doing this too soon.

But I know without a doubt that I have fallen for Kash. I know that because it hurts right now not being able to be with him.

I've never felt this way. Not even with Knight . . .

chapter
TWENTY-TWO

KASH

FUCK . . . LAST night really got to me in a way I wasn't expecting it to.

After Eden jumped in her jeep and took off, I sat in the parking lot for a good twenty minutes trying to get my head straight.

I thought long and hard about showing up at her doorstep and telling her the truth, hoping like hell she didn't slap me and then slam the door in my face, never wanting to see me again.

I'm in too deep with Eden to just let her walk away and forget I ever fucking existed all because I was a selfish prick, afraid of losing her over the truth.

She needs to know that I've been spending time with Alec for over six months and love the kid and care about his safety just as much as she does. I never want to see him hurt. Ever.

I was so damn close to telling her at the park, until she came out and told me she wasn't ready for Alec to know about me yet.

That messed me all up and even my fight wasn't enough to pull my head away from that shit.

My head wasn't into the fight at all last night. Not one damn bit.

It almost cost me my fight and then I would've been fucked on getting the money I need to buy the warehouse from Don. The big fight—that has now gotten pushed to next weekend— has a prize of ten grand so last night was important. You need to be ready at all times. Locations and dates always change when you least expect it. That's why I was even fighting last night to begin with. But I'll take what I can get.

I only need eight more grand since I've been saving for a while now, but I know it'll take years for me to save that kind of money with helping my sister out with rent and taking care of my place too.

The big fight will get me there next week instead.

But to tell you the truth, I'd give it all up for Eden anyway. But then where would that leave me?

Stripping to get by. I can't do that shit. Not if I want to be in her and Alec's lives.

That's why I need to be on top of my shit next week. There's no way in hell I'm letting Knight win. If anything, wanting to beat his ass for hurting Eden will be all the motivation I need to win.

He may have more experience and training, but I have more heart and I'll put every bit that I have into taking his ass down.

There's no way he's walking out of that ring without getting the fucking message.

Eden is mine and there's no way I'm allowing him to hurt her anymore. Her or Alec.

I just need for Eden to know that too.

And no matter how much it might hurt me in the long run, I'm letting her know tonight. Every little fucking detail. I don't matter. They do. If she leaves me to keep them both from hurting, then I'll take all the pain thrown at me.

I overslept this morning, apparently exhausted from my fight last night so it's now well into the afternoon.

It may be a little too late to bring Alec pancakes, but it's never too late to play with his new ball with him. I missed bringing him yesterday and it fucking hurt my heart. So here I am. And who knows if I'll get to see him again after this.

Without knocking, I walk into my sister's house to see Alec and Hannah coloring at the table. He looks bored and I can tell he's ready to get up move around.

I'm right, because a smile immediately takes over his little face the moment he notices me standing in the doorway. "Hunter!" He jumps up from the kitchen table and runs into my arms. "You made it today. Did you bring pancakes?"

I laugh and set him back down to his feet, feeling bad that I was too late for breakfast. "Not this time, little man. It's a little late for breakfast." I bend down and grab his shoulders. "Did you bring your new ball?"

He nods his head with excitement. "I did! It's in my backpack. I keep it in there."

"Okay good. Why don't you run and grab it and we'll play a little ball."

I stand up and lock eyes with Hannah from across the room after Alec rushes to the spare bedroom, excited to play.

"What the hell, Hunter?" she whisper yells. "You're dating Eden and you didn't tell me?" She rushes over to me and slaps my shoulder. "She doesn't know either, does she? She doesn't know you've been spending time with Alec?"

I shake my head, guilt taking over as I watch Alec drag his backpack over to the couch and begin digging through it. "Don't start, Hannah. I already know I'm a huge jerk for not telling her in the beginning. You think I wanted things to go this way? That

I expected to meet Alec's mother and fall for her? It just sort of happened."

She smiles slightly at the fact that I just admitted to falling for someone. Hannah knows more than anyone how hard it's always been for me to find a girl I truly want to be with. "Well when did you find out then?"

"I found out after we were already spending time together. I didn't know how to come out and tell her without scaring her off." I flex my jaw and watch as Alec runs out the door, yelling for me to follow him. "I was going to tell her last night but then she said she wasn't ready for us to meet yet. What the hell was I supposed to say to that?"

"I don't know . . ." She huffs and shakes her head. "I get it. Eden is tough when it comes to Alec. I know she's been hurt by his father and I know she's overprotective of Alec. But she's going to be really pissed and hurt once you finally tell her. Maybe you shouldn't worry about her not being ready and more worried about how upset and hurt she's going to be that you waited so long."

"Fuuuck." I run my hands through my hair, knowing she's right.

"Fuck is right. You better tell her today, big brother. She may be pissed for a while, but she'll eventually forgive you. I believe that because I've seen how happy she's been lately. It's the happiest I've seen her since I began watching Alec for her."

"I hope so." I push the screen door open and join Alec in the yard, knowing that my sister will most likely join us outside if she still wants to talk.

I just hope she doesn't because I'm already feeling really fucking emotional and I've never done well with my emotions.

Alec looks over as soon as I step outside and barely gives me enough time to stop, before he tosses the ball to me.

"Whoa!" I quickly reach out and catch it, pretending as if I'm about to fall over. "You've got a strong arm there, buddy. How about you be more careful next time so you don't hurt me."

Alec laughs and reaches out to catch the ball when I toss it back. "I don't think so, Hunter. You just need to be as strong as me. Maybe drink more milk?" He shrugs. "That's what mommy makes me drink to be strong."

"I'll try, buddy. I'll try . . ." I toss the ball back and he jumps into the grass to catch it.

"I almost missed it! Did you see how fast I am?" He jumps to his feet and runs around in a circle yelling about how fast he is.

"Yeah, but you're so fast that I almost missed it." I begin running as if I can't keep up with him and throw my arms up. "Throw it to me, bud. Just not too hard."

He gets ready to throw it to me but stops. "What happened to your face?" He tilts his head up and looks me over, just now noticing the bruises. "Did you get beat up?"

I laugh and shake my head. "Nah, I was stronger than the other guy. So maybe he needs milk too. Now throw me the ball."

"My daddy is strong too. He beats people up." He looks sad for a moment. "It's why he's never around."

My heart fucking breaks for him as he looks down at the ground and drops the ball.

"Hey. Hey." I run over and crouch down in front of him. "I'm here if you need me to be, buddy. Your daddy might be busy but I'll never be too busy for you, alright."

He smiles and looks up at me, his eyes filled with excitement. "For really?'"

"For really." I grab the ball and toss it up in the air before catching it. "Maybe I'll come around more often and we can hang out. Would you like that?"

"Yeees!" He jumps up and grabs the ball out of my hand,

before running around in a circle again. "Maybe you can come to my mommy's house. She's needs a friend too and we can all play!"

My heart jumps around in my chest at the thought of us all together. "Yes . . . maybe." I hold my hands out. "Ready?"

"Ready!"

I lose track of time while playing ball with Alec and forget about everything else that's been going on. I'm not sure how much time has gone by, but all that seems to matter right now is the smile on his little face.

That is until I look up to see Eden watching us from the driveway with a look of pure shock on her face. I was so zoned into playing with Alec that I didn't even notice her pull up.

"Eden . . ."

Holy fuck this is not how I wanted her to find out.

If there was any chance of her forgiving me for not telling her in the beginning, I'm pretty sure her finding out this way has ruined it . . .

Eden

I SWEAR I STOP BREATHING the moment I realize who Alec is playing with in Hannah's front yard. I'm not even sure how I missed his truck parked across the street, but I guess it's because I wasn't even thinking for one second that there'd be a possibility I'd see him here.

Not at my babysitter's house of all places.

Seeing Kash here confuses the hell out of me to the point that I find myself just standing here in a state of shock, watching them laugh and play as if they're close and have known each other for Alec's entire life.

The emotions running through me right now are so damn

confusing that I don't know if I want to scream or cry.

I'm angry because Kash clearly knows something he didn't tell me and overwhelmed with happiness at the sight of seeing the two men in my life that I care about the most spending time together.

I've imagined what it would be like when the two finally came face to face and here I am watching them interacting with so much love and happiness as if nothing else in the world matters right now.

My heart can't take the confusion. It hurts so damn bad.

"Eden . . ."

My heart drops to my stomach the moment Kash looks up, it clear on his face that he feels guilty, for me catching him here with Alec.

"What is this, Kash?" I take a step closer, trying my best to keep my composure as Alec comes running at me, excited to see me. I pick him up in my arms and force a smile, while glancing over his shoulder at Kash. "What are you doing here with my son?"

"He's my friend!" Alec says while jumping out of my arms. "Hunter. See I told you . . ." I watch with my teeth clenched as he rushes over and grabs Kash's hand, pulling him over to me. "Now we can all play. Mommy likes to play ball too but she's not as good as you are. We can teach her to be better!"

Kash flexes his jaw as his gaze meets mine. "I was going to tell you last night. I just didn't know how to bring it up."

"How long?" I question through tight lips, feeling as if my heart's about to beat out of my chest. "How long have you known?"

He goes to grab my hand, but I quickly pull it away, unsure of how to act right now. "Don't," I growl out. "Don't touch me."

A part of me wants to yell until he tells me the whole truth, while the other part wants to forgive Kash and believe he had good intentions for keeping this from me.

He looks hurt, but quickly hides it before Alec can catch on to the fact that we're upset with each other. He's still talking about baseball and making sound effects so I know he's not listening to our words, but his eyes catch on to emotions easily. "As soon as you told me your son's name."

I turn away and run my hands over my face, feeling like an idiot. He's been keeping it from me for longer than I thought. "Why didn't you tell me then? Dammit, Kash. I can't believe this right now."

"Alec . . ." Hannah appears on the front porch. She gives us both a sad look and motions for Alec to join her. "Come inside and pick out a popsicle. I'll even let you choose a flavor for me this time."

"Okay! I'll be back and then we can play." He releases both mine and Kash's hand and rushes up to the door to Hannah.

I wait until he's out of sight before turning back to Kash and losing it. "How the fuck could you do this to me, Kash? Or Hunter . . . whatever your name is. My son. My fucking son. You've been spending time with him behind my back, knowing that I wasn't ready for this. How could you *keep* this from me?"

His eyes look intense before he closes them and runs his hands down his face. "I was scared of losing you. That's why. Fuck!" He grips his hair in frustration, before attempting to touch me again, but I push him away. "I'm sorry." He throws his arms up, letting me know he won't touch me if I don't want him to. "I knew how much you wanted to protect Alec from getting hurt again and I felt that if you knew I'd been spending time with him for a while now that you'd freak out and push me away." He places his arms back down to his sides. "I'm sorry, Eden. You have no idea how bad it's been hurting me to keep this shit from you. The last thing I want to do is lie to you. I was a dick and there's nothing I wouldn't do to somehow make up for it."

My heart speeds up as I watch the pain and hurt takes over Kash's face. I want to forgive him right now. I want to be able to come out and say it's okay, but I can't. It's not. It's far from okay. "I seriously don't know what to say right now. I feel betrayed and that's not something I get over so easily. I need some time, Kash." My voice comes out harsh. "I'm sorry. I just can't think straight right now."

He leans his head back and tightly closes it eyes. "I'm sorry." He reaches out and cups my face, closing the distance between our bodies as if he can't stay away from me right now. "I can't lose you, Eden. Look at me." He tilts my chin up until our eyes lock. "The last thing I ever want to do is hurt you. That was never my intention and it fucking hurts so damn bad that I did that to you."

"You do realize this is one of the worse possible things you could've lied to me about, right?" I shake my head and attempt to push his hands away, but he just cups my face again, not giving up. "Kash. You fucking have my son playing ball with you. His favorite thing to do. He only ever does that with family. It's a family thing and now he's going to think you'll always be around for him. What am I supposed to do with that? Huh? Tell me!" I yell the last part, my emotions overwhelming me.

"Believe that I will be around. That I'm not fucking going anywhere. See that I'm not like that piece of shit who left you both without so much as thinking about how it would hurt you. That's where we're different. You and Alec are what matters to me. I could give a shit about myself. But I do care about not having you as mine. I do fucking care about not spending time with Alec ever again. I can't let that happen."

I close my eyes, finding it so easy to get lost in his touch. It's almost crazy the way a simple touch from him can unravel me.

"Mommy!"

I open my eyes to the sound of Alec's voice and quickly remove Kash's hands from my face, before he can begin asking me a bunch of questions that I'm not sure I'm able to answer right now.

I'm a fucking mess right now and the last thing I need is for Alec to see it.

"I've gotta go. I just . . ." I grab Alec's hand and begin walking him toward the jeep, trying my hardest not to cry.

"Where are we going?" Alec asks in a confused voice, while looking back at Kash. "I thought we were going to play with my new baseball."

It hurts my heart so damn bad to do this to him. But I need to deal with this situation when I have a clear head.

There's three people here I could hurt if I say the wrong thing. I just can't . . .

"Mommy took the rest of the day off work so we could visit grandpa at work and he can show you around the houses he's building. Doesn't that sound fun?"

I'm shitty for making this up on the spot, but it's the only thing that I know will make Alec forget about playing ball and leave without too many questions.

"But I want to play with Hunter, mommy. Can't we stay for a while longer?"

Kash puts on a smile and crouches down in front of him. He's trying his hardest to be strong but I can see the worry in his eyes. "Sorry, 'lil man. I have to get going now." He rubs the top of his head, before kissing it. "Be good for mommy and drink lots of milk so you can continue to be strong. Always be strong, okay?

Alec nods. "Okay. I can try . . ."

"I'll see you later, buddy."

"With pancakes?" Alec smiles up at him, waiting for his answer.

"Always . . ."

The ache I feel in my chest is unlike anything else when Alec throws his arms around Kash's neck and gives him a big hug. He's squeezing him so tightly that he's choking him, but it doesn't seem to bother Kash. "Bye, Hunter!"

"See ya, buddy."

I look back at Kash one last time, because truthfully, I have no idea when I'll be ready to see him again.

"I'm here if you ever need me," he says softly. "And I mean that. Just please don't walk away."

I don't know what to say to that so I don't say anything. I just hop in my jeep and take off, hoping with everything in me that I don't break down and cry in front of Alec.

That's exactly why I need to get him to my father so I can have a few minutes to myself and let it all out.

Kash kept the biggest secret from me that he ever could. Even his excuses might not be enough to ever fix this.

I have no idea how long it's going to take me to get over it. If I even can at all . . .

chapter
TWENTY-THREE

Eden

IT'S BEEN TEN DAYS SINCE I discovered Kash had been spending time with Alec behind my back and I have yet to be able to face him or accept his apology yet.

He's sent me one text message a day every day since then to check on me, but truthfully, I just don't know what to say to him. So I haven't responded to any of them.

I thought Kash was different. The last thing I was expecting was for him to lie to me and hide something so big. Even if it was only because he was afraid of losing me. He should've gave me the chance to figure out how him knowing Alec already would've made me feel.

This is the kind of behavior I'd expect from Knight and I just don't know what to do with that. Makes me wonder what else he could be hiding from me, although my whole body is telling me he would never hurt me on purpose.

What makes the whole situation even worse is that Alec's been asking about Hunter . . . Kash . . . I don't know what to call him anymore and I hate that.

After I took some time to calm down last week, I called and talked to Hannah about the situation and she assured me that she just pieced it all together the night I asked her to watch Alec so I could go to the club for a bit. She was just as clueless as I was.

I didn't want to punish Hannah for her brother's mistake so I told her she could continue to watch Alec just as long as Kash doesn't come by and see him anymore. For now at least.

"Hey! Can my right shoulder get a little damn attention, please?"

I pull out of the zone I'm in and focus my attention on my last client for the day. "Yeah, sorry."

Squirting more oil into my palms, I move over to the guy's right shoulder, just now realizing that I've spent the last fifteen minutes on the other one, while I was zoning out.

This client only has five minutes left and I have a feeling, I'll never see him on my table again after this session.

The timer goes off faster than I expected, causing the elderly man to groan out his displeasure.

"Well at least one shoulder will be nice and relaxed. As if my old ass isn't off balance as it is. Thanks for that."

"Sorry. If you want to lay back down I'll add ten minutes for free. I was zoning out, I admit it, and I apologize."

"Don't have time," he groans, while sitting up and throwing his sheet off, exposing himself. "Gotta pick my damn wife up from BINGO. I'll get my ass chewed out if I'm late."

"What the hell . . . thanks for the warning." I cover my face and blindly reach for the door.

"Well I didn't get a warning that this massage would suck as much as it did but sometimes life isn't fair, little girl."

I grip the handle and squeeze it, this old fucker beginning to piss me off. I apologized and offered to make up for it. What more does he want? "Fuck you, old man. Take your wrinkly balls and shit attitude and get the hell out of my room."

This has the old man laughing behind me as if me being an ass to him amuses him.

"Something funny, old man?"

"Yeah . . . finding out you have more balls than most men I deal with on the daily gives this *old man* something to smile about." He pauses for a second. "Thanks for that."

I feel his hand squeeze my shoulder, before I turn around to see him fully dressed. "See you next week, girl. Leave a spot open for me."

Not sure what to say, I just move out of the way and watch with a smile as he leaves my room.

"Seriously?" I burst into laughter, not sure what the hell just happened.

I can't seem to stop laughing, which only proves that my emotions are all over the place right now.

It takes me about twenty minutes to clean up for the day, before I meet up with Riley at the counter to clock out.

"You okay, babe?"

I nod my head and smile when I see she has Haven with her. "She's getting so big!" Haven laughs and swats my face when I bend down close to her.

"Sorry, she's in that phase where she just swings her arms everywhere."

"I remember those days with Alec. No need to apologize." I grab Haven's little fingers and smile down at her, hoping that something as cute as this little booger will help me forget about Kash for a moment.

It doesn't . . .

"Still not talking to Kash?" Riley finally comes out and asks.

I know she's been wanting to this entire week but has been

trying to spare my feelings by bringing him up. It's not hard to figure out that look of pity in her eyes every time she looks at me.

"No." I stand up and walk behind the desk to clock myself out. "I'm not ready yet. I just . . . I don't know how to forgive him for something so personal like that. He hurt me, Riley. Really bad."

"I know, babe." She looks away from Haven to look at me. "Look at it from his point of view," she says. "That's how you begin to forgive him and realize that he'd never do anything to hurt you on purpose. I think you'll understand more that way that he was just scared."

I look over at her with wide eyes as if I haven't thought of that myself. Maybe I did but hearing it from someone else just seems to make more sense.

"Kash has never been serious with a woman in the whole time I've known him. I've never seen him so scared to hurt or lose someone before." She stops and picks Haven up, holding her above her as she makes funny faces up at her. "Guys do crazy things when they're in love, Eden."

"In love?" My heart races at just the thought of Kash being in love with me.

"Yeah. In *love*. You don't know?" She smiles over at me. "Kash is in love. It's easy to see. Especially since he's been so miserable without you. He's barely left the house unless he has to and he's called off work at the club almost every night since you guys got into that fight last week. The couple nights he *did* work he refused to do any private dances and only made appearances in the club when it was his time on the stage. He spent the rest of the time in Cale's office talking about how much he misses you and Alec. Cale says it's been pretty painful to be around him. Last night was his last night. He's done with the club now."

There's an ache in my chest that is almost enough to make me burst into tears when I think about how miserable Kash has been.

I honestly didn't think me and Alec not being in his life would affect him the way it apparently has.

"I should go," I whisper, feeling overwhelmed again. "Knight is coming by to see Alec for a bit before his fight tonight. "I . . . um . . . I'll see you tomorrow."

I don't even give Riley a chance to speak before I rush out the door and to my jeep, needing to be alone as quickly as possible.

Finally letting my emotions out, I bury my face in my hands and burst into tears.

Being a mom isn't always easy. I know this. Making decisions for Alec and what's best in his life is so damn hard.

What if Kash being in it is the best thing for him? The best thing for both of us and I've just ruined it by shutting him out?

I sit here for ten minutes . . . maybe twenty before I finally compose myself enough to drive myself home.

Knight text me ten minutes ago and said he was at my place with Alec so he told Hannah she could leave.

I hate that Knight is already there. The last thing I need is for him to see how torn up I am over Kash right now.

Just something else for him to rub in my face and try to make me feel horrible about myself over.

When I pull up in the driveway, Knight is sitting on the porch and Alec is playing with the baseball Kash gave me to give to Alec that first night he took me out to the baseball field.

Knight looks up from his phone with a cocky grin when he sees me step out of my jeep. "Looks like showing my face was enough to show that asshole I wasn't going anywhere."

"What are you talking about?" My heart stops, nervous that

Knight did something to Kash that I don't know about.

"I have eyes, Eden. I see that he hasn't been around in days. Do you really fucking think that I haven't been watching him, making my face known to him?"

"You're an asshole." I look across the yard and smile at Alec as he tosses the ball up and down, playing by himself. "Don't cause a scene in front of my son, Knight."

"Don't have to." He stands up and places his hands on my shoulders, rubbing them. "He's out of the picture and that's all I wanted."

Feeling disgusted, I shake his hands from my shoulders and back away from him. "It's not because of you. Your face isn't as intimidating as you think. Trust me on that." I push past him and to the house. "Now go play with your son for once and leave me the fuck alone."

I begin shaking the moment I step inside.

What the hell did he mean by making his face known? Kash never mentioned to me any problems with Knight.

But knowing Kash he was probably just looking out for me.

"Shit." I lean against the wall, everything hitting me all at once.

All Kash wanted to do was protect me from the truth until he knew I was ready. I told him over and over again how Alec had been hurt by his father and he knew how scared I was to let another man into his life.

I can't really blame him for already knowing Alec ahead of time. He was stuck in a situation that he didn't know how to handle and I'm punishing him for that.

Is this how I should look at it?

Fuck, I don't know . . .

It's not even five minutes later that Knight barges his way into the house, looking pissed off. "You never gave Alec the gift I left for him?"

"Nope." I stand up and brush my hair out of my face. "You need to give it to him yourself. It's not my fault it's taken this long for you to come spend time with your son."

"Well where the fuck is it?" He rushes into the kitchen and begins pulling out drawers. "When I leave something here for my son you give it to him."

"No, I say firmly. "*You* come around enough to give it to him yourself."

He finally pulls the small box from the kitchen drawer I hid it in. "I'll give it to him myself right now, bitch."

"Fuck you, asshole," I say through clenched teeth. "Give it to him and leave. And by the way . . . I still need that child support money you promised. This is your last chance or I'm taking your ass to court and letting them deal with you."

He stops at the door and looks back at me. "Like I said before. You want the money you come and get it tonight after the fight."

With that he walks outside and slams the screen door shut.

I jump from the sound, my nerves all messed up right now.

This asshole must be crazy if he thinks I won't show up tonight for the money he owes me. I'm getting every last cent of the two grand he owes me for back child support.

A few minutes later, Knight speeds off and Alec comes rushing into the house, holding up a video game that he already owns.

"Daddy got me this game. I told him I already have it and he got upset." He gives me a sad look and runs into my arms. "I miss Hunter, mommy. He always played with me and knew all the games I have. Where is Hunter? He hasn't come to Hannah's to bring me pancakes anymore. Did I do something wrong?"

My heart drops to my stomach when I hear the pain in his

voice. I hate it so damn much and I hate that I'm the reason Kash isn't in his life right now.

I'm so scared right now, but I think now is the time I tell him the truth.

"No, baby boy. Never. Don't even think you did something wrong." I crouch down in front of him. "Mommy cares about Hunter in the same way I cared about your father. Something happened and I asked him to stay away for a bit. I'm so sorry, baby."

A tear falls from his eye that he quickly swipes away. "Are you mad at Hunter, mommy? Don't be mad at my friend. He's my only friend. I miss him."

His bottom lip begins to quiver so I quickly pull him into my arms, wanting nothing more than to stop the tears from coming.

Kash not being in our lives is hurting the both of us and I hate it. Alec just hasn't been the same since the first day Kash didn't show up at Hannah's when he was expecting him.

"You'll see him soon, baby." I rub the back of his head, before kissing it. "He misses you too. I promise you that. I'll fix it, baby. I'll fix it . . ."

Alec must be exhausted, because I feel him going slack in my arms the more I rub the back of his head.

Picking him up, I carry him to his room and place him in bed.

I wait until he's asleep, before leaving him alone in his room and shutting the door behind me.

Sitting here alone on the couch, my thoughts go back to Kash and that little ache in my chest returns and this empty feeling fills my stomach.

I find myself staring at my phone for a few minutes, before I pull up his number and type out a message. I need to fix this. To fix us.

Eden: Can we talk tonight?

I just hope I haven't waited too long . . .

chapter
TWENTY-FOUR

KASH

IT'S BEEN TEN DAYS SINCE I've seen or spoken to Eden and Alec and it's fucking with me big time, sending me into a depression I haven't felt since losing my father.

I've been doing everything I can to try not to think about how bad it fucking hurts losing them, but it's the only thing that matters to me now.

The only thing that's been slightly distracting is my constant training for the fight that's happening in less than ten minutes.

I don't even give a shit about the money at this point. All I want to do is fuck Knight up for placing his hands on Eden and treating his family like they don't matter.

Family is everything and he has one that means the world to me. I'd give anything to have them as my own.

"Fuuuuck!" I swing out and punch the bag one last time, before grabbing it and fighting to catch my breath.

"You're good, man," Calvin grips my shoulder and hands me a bottle of water. "You're taking this motherfucker down.

Don't even sweat it."

"I'm not," I grit out. "I'm just getting my head in the right place and trying to keep it there."

Abe laughs from the doorway. "He's going crazy right now, breaking stuff and shit. He just realized Hunter Knight is *you* because of the poster on the wall. I've never seen him so worked up about a fight before. This is fucking awesome."

I broke down and told the guys *everything* a few days ago. The whole damn situation. I had no choice. They could tell I was fucked up.

I grin and crack my neck, before pouring water over my head. "Good. I want him worked up for our fight. It'll feel that much better when I take everything from him."

I take a seat on the old worn out couch and close my eyes, getting lost in thought as Calvin re-wraps my hands for me.

I may have been giving Eden space, but doesn't mean for one fucking second that I've given up. That's something I'll never do when it comes to her. When it comes to *them*.

Even if it takes a year, I'm not going anywhere. I already promised her that and I don't break promises.

"Hey, bro. You're bag's vibrating. Want me to get it?"

I open my eyes and look up at Abe, who's holding my gym bag. "Nah. I can't have any kind of distractions right now. It's probably just one of the guys checking on me for the hundredth time this week. Leave it."

Abe shrugs and tosses my bag back down. "Knight may not lose fights but he *is* tonight. Don't let his experience in the ring intimidate you. Fight with your heart. Just like you taught us. From what I can tell, man, he doesn't have much of one."

I nod and jump to my feet, getting myself pumped up as we begin making our way to the main event.

There's people scattered all around this place, in the

hallways, in the rooms with other fighters that fought earlier, but the main event is packed full. There's barely even room to stand without being shoulder to shoulder.

This is the craziest shit I've ever seen.

But when you fight without rules, it brings curious people in. Everyone wants to see someone get hurt and everyone wants to bet on who that person is going to be.

I know I should be nervous, because a lot is riding on me winning, but I'm not. I'm pumped up and ready to take this asshole out. He's got me all fired up. Has for a while now.

Flexing my jaw, I make my way to the middle of the room where the ring is. Adrenaline pumps through my veins the moment I look out into the crowd, listening to the cheers of excitement.

I know most of them are here for Knight because he's well known, but I don't let that mess with my head.

I keep my gaze straight ahead, never taking it off Knight as he pushes his way through the crowd and jumps between the ropes with a cocky grin on his face.

He thinks he has me. That this is the moment he's been waiting for. He's been following me around for days, keeping an eye on me, and now I'm exactly where he wants me: In his territory.

That shit doesn't intimidate me.

My eyes meet his and lock as we both start to circle around each other, waiting for the signal to fight.

I'm so zoned in on Knight, thinking of all the ways I want to make him hurt, that I don't even hear the announcer, until the bell dings, indicating that the fight has started.

Knight cracks his neck and begins hopping in place, showing me how pumped up he is. "Unlike last time, I'm ready motherfucker. This will teach you to stay away from what is mine."

Not letting his little trash talk get to me, I swing out, hitting Knight with a right hook. He stumbles back, not expecting it and spits out blood.

I smirk as he wipes his lip off and growls at me. "Are you sure about that?"

"Fuck you!" he bites out, while swinging out with his right foot, knocking me off balance. He takes this as an opportunity to dig into my ribs, pushing me against the ropes with his body weight.

The crowd begins cheering Knight on, only giving him more confidence that he can take me, but I manage to grab the back of his head and connect my knee to his face, putting all my anger in the blow.

Blood gushes down his face, dripping down my knee, only making the blow feel that much fucking better.

I grab his hair and yank his head back so he's looking at me. "Never fucking hurt the people I care about, motherfucker. Touch her again and your dead. That's a fucking promise." Rage courses through me as the words leave my mouth. "I keep my promises."

With that I release his hair and swing my fist up, connecting it with his chin. He falls back, but quickly makes his way back to his feet.

The way he's looking at me right now, as if he's got the right to touch Eden anyway he pleases, only makes me want to rip his throat out more.

The only reason I didn't come after him the moment I found out about him hurting her, was because I knew this moment would come. There was no way I wasn't letting it be us in this ring tonight.

He takes his eyes off me and turns around to face the crowd. He runs his arm over his face and grabs the ropes, screaming out in anger. Then he comes at me, slamming me against the other set of ropes with his body weight, before punching me in the ribs a few times and then the side of my head.

He continues to take jabs at me, but he's becoming winded. I can feel it, so I push him away, allowing us both to return to the middle of the ring.

We circle around each other a few times before Knight comes at me, diving for my legs, but I grab onto his neck and plow my knee into his head twice, allowing him to fall back.

I stand above him, knowing damn well that I can finish him here and now, but I'm not done with his ass yet. Not until I know he gets the fucking message.

Taking a slow breath, I look away from Knight and into the crowd when a group of women begin screaming my name, cheering me on. Everything around me stops the moment my eyes land on Eden pushing her way toward the ring.

Knight must notice who I'm staring at, because before I know it, he comes at me and captures me in a headlock. "Looks like she came here to see me after all," he growls into my ear, before kneeing me in the stomach and bending down to speak in my ear again. "She'll always be mine. I was her first and I'll be her last." He takes another swing to my ribs, before pushing me over.

I place my hands on the mat and get ready to push myself up, but get lost in Eden the moment our eyes meet.

Her eyes widen as if she's just now noticed me as she continues to push her way through the crowd to get closer to the ring.

Before I know it, Knight kicks me in the face, knocking me back down to my side. It stings like hell, but I push past it and jump to my feet, him not expecting me to recover so quickly.

This is it. I'm done playing this little game with him in the ring. This is the moment he learns not to fuck with what I love.

Grabbing the back of his head with both hands I push his head down and lift my knee, plowing it straight into his face between the eyes. I don't give him a chance to recover, before my fist connects with his face over and over again, all my rage going into the blows.

As soon as I release his head, he falls back, knocked out cold.

There's a mixture of cheers and boos throughout the crowd, but the only thing I'm focused on is Eden climbing between the ropes and running toward me.

I have no idea what to expect. Especially since I never told her about my fighting, but I can't deny that seeing her is the happiest I've been in over a week.

She stops in front of me and grabs my face, before throwing her arms around my neck and kissing me long and hard as if she's missed me just as much as I've missed her.

Her heavy breathing hits my lips as she pulls away and looks my face over, taking in the blood and bruises. "Shit, Kash! Your face. Are you okay?"

"Don't worry about my face. I'm so fucking sorry, baby." I pull her into my arms and place my forehead to hers, locking my gaze on hers. Looking into her eyes is all it takes to calm me and help me breathe again. "I didn't tell you because I didn't want you to think I was anything like that piece of shit. This was my last fight. I promise. I only needed the money for my gym and–"

"I don't care," she says cutting me off. Her arms tighten around my neck as if she's desperate to feel me next to her. "I know you're nothing like Knight. That's all I've been thinking about for days. I texted you a bit ago because I miss you. I've missed you so damn much. So has Alec. I don't care anymore. We *need* you."

My heart fucking jumps all over the place with excitement. I smile against her lips, before cupping her face and slamming my lips against hers again, desperate to show her how much I need her.

I don't even notice Knight being helped up by a couple of his guys, until he pushes one of them down and growls out his anger. "Don't fucking touch me. Get off me."

Wanting to protect Eden, I push her behind me and watch as Knight gets up to his feet.

"So that's how it's going to fucking be, Eden?"

I wait until he's steady and looking at us, before I get up in his face. "Never fucking hurt *my* family again. I plan to take care of them in ways you'll never be capable of." I grab the back of his head and growl the last part in his ear. "I'm not going *anywhere.*"

Walking away from him before I lose my shit again, I pick Eden up and carry her out of the ring and through the crowd, not setting her down until we're in the hallway.

Then I slowly back her against the wall and pin her body against it with my sweaty one. I just stare into her eyes for a few minutes, letting her see how much I fucking care. "I love you, Eden. You may still be pissed at me for a while but I promise to do everything in my power to make up for it. I'll never lie to you again and that's a promise. You and Alec mean the world to me. I don't need months or years to figure that shit out. I've been a miserable asshole without you two."

She smiles against my lips and grips my face. "Do you mean that?"

I rub my hands over her head and nod. "With everything in me."

"I was scared, Kash. Scared of getting hurt and making it possible for Alec to get her too. It's my job to protect him. When I caught you two playing and having fun together I knew there was *nothing* I could do to protect him at that point if you were to walk out of his life. I freaked, unsure of what to do." She runs her fingertips over my lips, causing me to close my eyes. "I knew at that very moment that Alec and I were both in too deep with you. That we both had fallen. I love you, Kash . . . Hunter . . . I don't care. I'll call you anything you want, but I love you. I don't want to feel the pain I've felt for the last week anymore. I've realized that letting you in and risking possibly getting hurt in the long run is far better than not having you in our lives. I want to give us a chance. I want you in our lives. No more secrets."

Fuck, my heart is beating so fast that it hurts right now. I never thought words could be so powerful until this very moment.

I hear footsteps behind us, before Abe speaks. "Holy fuck that was intense!"

"Give us a few," I growl. "Or maybe thirty."

Grabbing Eden's legs, I lift her up and wrap them around my waist.

I desperately need to be alone with her right now. It's been too long since I've been able to touch her.

Making my way down the hall, I quickly push the door open to the room I've been in all day and shut it behind me.

Claiming her mouth with mine, I fall back onto the couch and pull her body up so that she's straddling me.

I growl out in surprise when she bites my lip and reaches in between us to undo my jeans. "I've missed you inside me, Kash. I want to feel you. Only you . . ."

Letting her pull my cock out, I wrap my hands into the back of her hair and pull back as she pulls her dress up, pushes her panties aside and slides down onto my cock.

We both moan out at the feel of me being inside of her. I hope like hell that I never have to go without this feeling ever again.

It's not just the physical pleasure, it's so much more than

that. It's the way I feel inside knowing that she's mine and I'm the only one being inside of her this way.

I fucking love it.

We get lost in each other, her riding me slow and deep, our mouths barely ever separating expect for me trailing kisses over her neck and whispering in her ear that she's mine.

We may be in the back of a damn training gym with a shit ton of people in the building, but none of that matters to us right now.

It feels like it's just the two of us.

I feel her body begin to shake above mine as if she's getting close to reaching orgasm, so I grab her hips and take control, sucking her bottom lip into my mouth as she comes undone above me.

This has me holding her down onto my cock, releasing myself as deep inside her as I can as I look into her eyes.

"Holy shit . . . Kash." She places her forehead to mine, while fighting to catch her breath. "That was amazing."

"I know, baby." I pull her in for a kiss and she smiles against my lips.

"Are you being cocky?"

I laugh and grab the back of her head. "No. I didn't mean it in that way. Although . . ."

We both just stay this way for a while, neither one of us wanting to move.

That is until one of my idiot friends knock on the door.

"Fuck me . . ."

"Already did," Eden says with a grin. "See I can do it too."

I grip her hips and lift her off me, kissing her one last time before standing up and grabbing something to clean her off with. "That's why we're perfect for each other."

Grunting, I open the door to Abe and Calvin pushing their

way inside.

Calvin gives me a slap on the back and shakes me with excitement. "Good shit, man. I've never seen that look on Knight's face before." He turns to Eden and smiles. "You came at just the right time."

Abe comes up behind Eden and drapes an arm over her shoulder. "So I heard you're friends with Hannah . . ."

"Don't even think about it, dick." I grab Eden away from Abe and kiss her. "Don't put in a good word for him. He's an idiot."

Abe shrugs and hands me an envelope. "I collected this for you, man. Congratulations. You've got your own training gym now."

Eden's smile widens as she wraps her arms around my neck. "Congratulations, baby."

"Fuck yes!" I pick her up and kiss her hard. "Let's get you home to Alec."

Eden gives me a confused look when I set her down and grab her hand. "Aren't you staying to celebrate?"

I shake my head and run my thumb over her cheek. "Don't need to. You and Alec are the only ones I need to celebrate with and since Alec is sleeping . . ." I lean in to speak against her lips. "We can celebrate alone until you kick me out."

"Maybe I won't kick you out this time . . ."

Those are the exact words I needed to hear tonight after being away from Eden for this long.

"Fuck, baby. Now I'm really ready to get out of here."

Before anyone can stop us, I grab my shit and escape out the back door with Eden.

The moment we pull up at her house and she drags me along behind her to her bedroom, I know it's going to be one of the best nights of my life.

Here with her is where I want to be. Nothing else matters but being with her.

From here on out, I'm doing everything in my power to prove to her she's my world. Both her and Alec . . .

chapter
TWENTY-FIVE

Eden

I WAKE UP AND ROLL over, running my hand over the empty mattress beside me.

Even though Kash is gone, I can't help the smile that takes over at the memory of him sleeping in my bed last night.

Laying in the safety of his strong arms; resting my head on his chest, made me realize I've never really felt as safe and cared for as I do when I'm with Kash.

It was comforting knowing that when I woke up in the middle of the night that I'd feel him against me, our bodies tangled together beneath the sheets.

The fact that he kissed me every chance he got and whispered in my ear how much he loved me and missed made me feel more at ease that I followed my heart and let him back in.

I know without a doubt that Kash is the only man able to break down my walls and make me feel as much as I do.

There's a small ache in my chest that he was gone before I woke, even though I knew to expect it.

Right before we started dozing off, he set his alarm for early this morning, wanting to make sure he took off before Alec woke up.

It's probably better this way so that the first time Alec doesn't see us together is in my bed, wrapped in each other's arms.

I have so much respect for Kash for thinking of Alec over anything else. That's exactly the kind of man he needs in his life. Someone who will put him first even over us.

With a smile on my face, I sit up and grab my phone, checking to see if Kash sent me a message after he left.

Uneasiness fills my stomach when I see ten missed text messages from Knight. I'm sure he spent the night freaking out after we left him in the ring. Probably drinking and complaining to all his little friends how I chose someone else over him for once.

Doesn't bother me one bit. He deserved every bit of what he got.

Knight is no longer my problem. Come Monday I'm looking into lawyers and taking him to court for child support and letting them deal with everything else involving Knight and him being in Alec's life.

I will not allow him to hurt my son anymore. I've given him all the time in the world and he has yet to change. His time is up.

"Mommy . . ." Alec appears in the doorway with tired eyes and messy hair. "I had a nightmare. I don't want to go back to sleep. Can I lay with you?"

I frown and hold my arms out. "Come here, baby boy. Mommy will keep you safe." I wrap my arms around him and rub the top of his head when he crawls into the bed next to me. "Never forget that."

"Are you strong enough mommy? You don't have big muscles like some of the monsters." He looks up at me, waiting for an answer.

I smile and kiss his forehead. "Being strong enough for you is my whole reason for living, baby. That and loving you. I'll take down anyone who hurts you."

"Love you too, mommy." He sits up on his knees and wraps his arms around my neck, before kissing my forehead just like I just did to him. "Is it because you drink lots of milk like me?"

I laugh and grab his face, kissing his nose. "Yes, baby. That's part of the reason I'm so strong."

Alec and I both look toward the hallway, when the front door opens and someone steps inside.

There's only three people who would be inside my house this early and without knocking. My father, Knight or Kash, although I'm not sure Kash plans on coming back this morning without talking to me first.

It almost sounds like someone is digging through some kind of plastic bags and pulling things out.

This instantly has Alec's ears perking up, before he jumps out of bed and runs toward the hallway as if he's very familiar with the sounds he's hearing.

I quickly run after him, my heart speeding up when I notice Kash standing in the kitchen, unzipping his hoodie as if it's so natural for him to be here bringing breakfast for me and Alec.

Alec notices him at the same time and his eyes light up. I can't deny that mine do too.

"Hunter!" He rushes through the kitchen with the biggest smile on his face I've seen in a long time. "You came and brought me pancakes?"

Kash reaches out to give Alec a high five, Kash pretending to miss his hand a few times, before they finally connect hands and he pulls him in for a quick hug. "Of course, buddy." He looks over Alec's head and winks at me. "I told you I'd always bring you pancakes. I keep my promises. I'm not going anywhere."

Alec turns to me with excitement and grabs my hand, dragging me over to the table. "Mommy! Hunter came back! He brought pancakes just like at Hannah's. You were right. He's not mad at me."

Kash makes a pained face as if Alec's words just shot him straight through the heart. He quickly turns away as if he's trying to hide his emotions from us.

Shows me right here just how much he truly does love Alec.

I sniff the air, trying to lighten the mood. "I can smell them, baby. Mmmm . . . mommy's starving. I'll try to save you one, but I can't make any promises."

Alec's mouth drops open as he looks up at me. "You're not going to save me any!"

Kash laughs and pulls out a kitchen chair for Alec, before setting a plate down in front of him. "I got you, little man. All the pancakes your little heart desires right here on this plate. I'll even get you more if you really want."

Alec looks over and sticks his tongue out at me. "Ha! I don't need to worry. Hunter will get me more. Eat all you want to, mommy. Doesn't matter."

I stick my tongue back out at him, before tickling him so hard that he almost falls out of his chair with laughter.

When I turn to Kash he's smiling bigger than I've ever seen him smile before.

"Thank you for doing this." I watch as he sets a plate of pancakes in front of me." You really didn't have to."

"I do this because I want to, Eden. I do it because it makes me happy. It's always made me happy bringing Alec pancakes and spending time with him." He tilts my chin up and kisses me. "You both make me happy and I'd do this every day if it made the two of you happy."

My heart does this little flutter and a smile takes over that I can't hide. I'm pretty sure it's bigger than the one Kash just had on his face.

This man makes me happy and from the look on Alec's face right now and the look I saw on his face last week when they placed together; he makes Alec happy too.

I can't ask for anything more than that.

KASH

Spending the night with Eden wrapped in my arms last night was far more fulfilling than earning the rest of the money needed for my gym.

Yeah it felt good as hell knowing I have everything I need to get it up and running after all these years, but knowing that I was the man holding Eden in my arms as she curled into my chest made my life feel so damn complete.

It hurt leaving her this morning, but I did it for Alec. I wanted him to see me the right way. The same way he's always seen me.

I knew showing up with pancakes like I do at Hannah's would be a simple way to show him I'm not going anywhere. Just like I haven't for the last six month.

Alec knew he'd see me every week and now I'm hoping he'll get to see me every day.

Once we're all done eating and just playing with Alec at the table, Eden's phone rings, so she grabs it and walks into the living room to answer it.

I sit with Alec and listen to his talk about his video games and how his daddy brought him LEGO Star Wars. Of course that dick wouldn't pay enough attention to him to know he already owned it.

"Well you know what . . ." I pull Alec's chair out and clean begin cleaning up the table. "How about sometime this week we go and get LEGO Batman. You still want that, "lil man?"

He nods his head and begins making sound effects like he's driving the Batmobile.

"Done deal then, buddy."

When I look up, Eden is standing in the doorway watching me with a smile.

"I'm so glad you came back." She walks into the kitchen and wraps her arms around my neck. "I hated waking up to you being gone."

I run my thumb over her bottom lip, before kissing her. "I hated leaving too. I hope with everything in me that I don't have to do that again."

She shakes her head. "I don't want you to have to. I want Alec to know how much I love you."

Alec's head suddenly pops up, between us. "Mommy you said you love Hunter. Does that mean he doesn't have to stay away no more?"

Eden smiles at me, before she rubs the top of Alec's head. "Nope, baby. Kash is welcome to see us anytime he wants."

Alec makes a funny face and looks up at me. "Kash? Who's that?"

I laugh and rub his head. "It's what a lot of people call me. Pretty cool, huh? Like money."

"That is pretty cool. Can I call you that, too?"

"You bet, 'lil man. Whatever makes you happy."

Eden waits until Alec zooms out of the kitchen before she wraps her arms around my neck again and smiles. "That was my dad on the phone. I forgot that I told him that Alec and I were going to visit him today. I'm not sure what your plans are . . ."

"My plans are whatever you want them to be, Eden." I pull her bottom lip into my mouth, before releasing it with a smile. "I was hoping to take you and Alec to play some ball, but I'm wherever you want to be."

"Would you mind if my dad stops by the park? If not then I can just visit him later. He won't mind-"

"I'm okay with meeting your dad, Eden. Like I said . . ." I lean in and press my lips below her ear. "I'm not going anywhere."

She laughs as Alec runs past us and I reach out and mess up his hair. "Good. I was hoping you'd say that. And we should probably choose a different park to go to . . ."

I let out a small growl, thinking about that night. "We'll keep that park to ourselves. I have one in mind for us to take Alec too."

It's the one my father always took me to as a kid. Now I want to take Alec there.

Eden looks at me and stiffens up, immediately looking worried when the front door opens to someone stepping inside.

On instinct, I push Eden behind me and look around the corner to see who's inside the living room.

Rage courses through me when my gaze lands on Knight walking toward Alec, who is now sitting on the couch.

"You really think it's smart to show up here unannounced?" I step into the living room and clench my jaw, not taking my eyes off Knight. "I'm pretty sure you don't live here."

He looks surprised for a second as if he's just now noticed I was here, before his face turns to pure anger. Apparently, he missed a big ass truck parked in front of the house.

"It's none of your damn concern. I'm here to take my son. I don't want him around another man." He turns back to Alec and holds his arms out. "Come with daddy. We're leaving."

"You're not taking *my* son." Eden gets ready to push past me, but I place my hand on her arm, letting her know I'll take care of her and Alec. I'll always take care of them.

"The hell you are," I growl out. "Come here, Alec."

Alec stands up and looks back and forth between myself and Knight, as if he doesn't know what to do, before finally running into my arms and burying his face in my shoulder.

"Leave, Knight," Eden says from beside us. "You have no right to be here. I won't tell you again."

"No, fuck that!" He grabs for the coffee table and flips it over, causing Alec to whine and grab onto me tighter. "You're *my* family. Not his. What the fuck, Eden. This is bullshit."

As much as I would like to rip Knight's throat out for acting this way in front of Alec, I know I need to keep my cool. Violence is the last thing I want it to come down to.

"I'm asking you not to do that in front of Alec. If I have to ask you again, then we're going to have to step outside and handle this like men."

"I'm done playing games," Eden adds, while rubbing Alec's back to comfort him. "You've got five seconds to get out of my house or I'm calling the cops."

He looks shocked from Eden's threat. As if he didn't think she'd ever get the law involved. "You know what. Fuck this shit. You can have the two of them. I don't want them anymore."

Eden releases a relieved breath the moment Knight rushes outside and speeds off in his car.

I turn to her and kiss the side of her head. "You okay, babe?"

She nods and grabs both mine and Alec's arm. "Yeah. I'm good." She kisses Alec's arm and then rubs it. "Daddy won't ever act that way around you again. I promise."

I look down at Alec when he raises his head to look up at me. "Was I strong, Kash?"

I smile and push his hair out of his eyes. "Yeah, 'lil man. You were strong." I set Alec down and turn to Eden. "Come on. We need some time to cool off. Leave the table and I'll clean it up when we get back. Okay?"

She nods her head. "Yes. I like that idea."

It took everything in me to keep my composure the way I did, but I can assure you I would've liked to kill him there on the spot.

Now I'm taking Alec and Eden out for a day they both deserve. Knight will be forgotten soon enough . . .

chapter
TWENTY-SIX

Eden

IT SEEMS ALEC HAS ALREADY forgotten about the huge scene Knight made back at the house.

We've been at the park for an hour, the three of us playing ball as if we're a family. My heart has never been so damn happy. This is exactly the kind of childhood I wanted Alec to have.

Two people who care about him, playing and spending time with him, like he matters.

Alec deserves a man in his life who wants to do things with him. Seeing Kash and how he treats Alec as if he's his own son has me so happy that it hurts.

Seriously, my face hurts from smiling so much.

I'm just sitting back, taking a break from playing ball when I hear footsteps in the grass beside me.

My heart does a little happy dance when I see my father standing beside me, watching Kash and Alec with a smile on his face.

It's been a while since he's seen Alec so carefree and fun

with anyone besides the two of us.

"This is the guy you've been telling me about?"

"Yes. He's so good with Alec that I seriously have no words, dad. They've been spending time together all morning and afternoon. It makes me so undeniably happy."

"Hey." He reaches for my hand and helps me up to my feet. "Makes your old man happy, too. I knew that piece of shit father of his would never do these types of things with him. I just hope you're sure he's going to stick around and not hurt Alec."

I turn away from my dad and laugh as Kash hits the ball and then picks Alec up and begins running to first base with him.

The look on Alec's face is pure happiness.

"You see that?"

My dad nods. "Yeah, I do."

"That tells me that he's not going anywhere. I have to listen to my heart and that's exactly what I plan to do."

"You love him?"

"I do. A lot more than I ever imagined I could in such a short time. Everything I do is for Alec and I believe he needs Kash just as much as I do." I turn back to face my dad again to see him smiling at me.

"I haven't seen you this happy in a long time, baby girl. So I'm going to trust this Kash guy is going to take care of your heart better than Knight did."

Just then Kash looks up at us. He freezes for a second, before pointing up the hill to show Alec who's just joined us.

I can tell Kash is a little nervous but he waits for Alec to take off running before he walks up the hill, behind him, trying to keep his cool.

He waits for my dad to get done hugging Alec, before he reaches out to shake his hand. "It's good meeting you, sir. I admire how much you love and take care of your daughter and grandson. Reminds me a lot of how my father would be if he were still around."

My chest aches at the reminder of Kash losing his father. I lost my mother too but it was from her running off when I was young. I can't even imagine his loss.

"It's nice to meet you too, young man." My dad gives him a sympathetic look and gives his hand a pat. "I'm sorry to hear you lost your father. He sounds like he was a good man and from what I hear from my daughter . . . you are too."

"Thank you, sir. I do my best." He smiles. "You here to play some ball? There's always room for one more."

My dad shakes his head releases Kash's hand finally. "Not today. Just wanted to swing by and meet the guy my daughter's been telling me about for the last couple weeks."

"Okay, I'm ready to play again!"

Kash smiles and tosses the ball up to Alec when he begins bouncing around with energy.

"Looks like I've got a kid to play with." Kash reaches out and grabs my father's shoulder. "I hope to see you again soon. For longer next time."

"Me too," my father says with a sincere smile. "Take care of my daughter and grandson until then. That's all I ask."

"That's all I want," Kash responds. He leans in and kisses me on the forehead. "We'll meet you on the field, babe."

Happiness fills me as I watch Kash run down after Alec, them stopping every so often to toss the ball back and forth to each other.

"I have to say I'm impressed with this young man." He kisses my forehead. "I should get going. My guys are a little behind so I've got to light a fire under their asses to get this job done."

"Alright, dad." He gets ready to walk away, but I stop him. "Thank you, dad."

"For what?"

"For always talking care of us. Just like Kash said. I know I haven't really told you how much it means to me."

"You're my baby. Always will be."

I smile and watch him walk away, before I make my way over to where Kash is pitching the ball for Alec.

"Way to go!" I scream when Alec hits the ball across the field. "Wooo!"

Alec gets a big grin on his face as he takes off running to first base.

"Your turn, momma." Kash winks and tosses the ball up, before catching it. "I'll take it easy on you."

"Yeah!" Alec yells. "Come on, mommy. You can hit it too."

I narrow my eyes at Kash and pick up the bat, getting into stance. "Oh I know I'll hit it. I'm not worried. Just wanted to let you boys warm up first."

"Is that it?" Kash asks with an amused smile. "Someone being Mrs. Cocky now?"

I lift a brow. "Maybe you rubbed off on me."

"I love that." Kash says with a grin.

"Hurry and throw the ball!" Alec yells. "I'm ready to win!"

"Alright." Kash winds up before pitching the ball.

Both boys look at me with wide eyes when the bat smashes the ball across the park.

This has me doing a little happy dance all the way to first base.

I know this is just the beginning, but I'm hoping with everything in me that things stay this way for as long as possible.

Kash being here makes everything feel so complete. Makes me believe that everything in this world is A-Okay.

I never thought that feeling was possible until him . . .

EPILOGUE

KASH

SIX MONTHS LATER . . .

"RIGHT HERE, BUDDY." I'M CROUCHED down in front of Alec, holding my forearms up for him to punch. "A few more times. You're almost done."

Alec does as told, letting out a grunt with each impact. The face he's making is of pure concentration.

"Good. Now elbows."

"I'm so strong, Kash!"

"Yeah you are, "lil man. Pretty soon you might be able to take me."

I pull the sparring pads off my forearms and grab Alec's head, resting my forehead to his. "I'm proud of you. Love you, bud."

"Love you too, Kash." He smiles when I mess up his hair. "Watch this."

I stand up and watch with a proud smile as Alec begins punching and elbowing the air.

The sound effects only make it that much better to watch. I don't remember ever being as good with that when I was a kid and my father taught me how to fight.

I love knowing that I'm the one who taught Alec everything he knows about fighting and self-defense. Makes me feel like my father. He was the greatest man I ever knew and it's because of him I know how to be a father to Alec right now.

"You two behaving?"

We both look over at the sound of Eden's voice.

My heart still goes crazy at the sight of her even after all these months. I'm pretty positive it's only gotten more intense as time has passed.

Alec runs around in a circle and begins punching the air again. "Watch this, mommy! Kash says I'll be able to take him soon."

A huge smile spreads over Eden's face as she watches her son go all crazy on the air like nothing in this world can hold him down. "Good job, baby boy. Just remember what you promised me, okay?"

"I know!" He stops punching the air and runs over to give Eden a hug. "I promise not to hit anyone."

She grabs his head and kisses it. "And I know you'll keep that promise. Remember how Kash taught you the importance of keeping promises?"

He nods his head. "Yes, mommy. Kash is a good teacher. First baseball and now fighting. I'm going to be so cool!"

I laugh and walk over to take Alec's gloves off. "So cool, kid. Now why don't you run over and have a snack before we take off."

As soon as Alec runs out of the room, headed to the snack area, I grab Eden's waist and pull her against me. "Fuck, baby. I've missed you all day."

She grins and wraps her arms around my neck, pulling me down to her. "Looks like you and Alec have been having fun running this place together though. I'm sure you can't miss me that much."

I growl and pull her bottom lip into my mouth. "If Alec weren't here, I'd show you just how much. I'm sure you'd believe me then."

She places her hands to my chest and laughs when I run my short beard over her neck, teasing her. "As much as I wish we had time for this . . ." She tugs on my beard, pulling me in for a kiss. "The others are waiting on us. Styx has already started the grill and Meadow has sent me three texts telling us to hurry before the guys lose their shit. Apparently, they're starving."

"Fuck me," I growl. "They can start without us. They're not going to miss us if we're twenty or forty minutes late or so. I'll let you choose which room. Alec will be busy with snacks for a while. He won't even notice we're gone."

"And let him empty out the snack stash?" She shakes her head and begins backing away with a grin. "Why don't you get this place closed down and Alec and I will meet you at Cale's. Riley has already text me that she's home."

I grunt and run my hands down my sweaty face. "Alright, babe. But you're mine after this little cookout and Alec falls asleep. We're both turning our phones off and I'm dedicating all my energy into making you scream my name."

She laughs when I lift a brow and slap her ass.

"I'm serious, babe. Our friends barely give us any alone time anymore. I'm desperate to get you to myself. No fucking lie."

I grab her hand, before she can get too far away and pull her back against me. "Kash, we've gotta go!" She closes her eyes and moans when I run my tongue over her lips. "Okay," she breathes. "Our phones are going off after this cookout. I promise."

"I knew you'd say that," I tease. "You never can resist my mouth."

"That's not a lie." She kisses my neck and turns away. "See you there."

I push down on my erection and watch as she walks away, that perfect ass of hers swaying in front of me.

I only seem to want her more with each day we spend together and to be honest, I've never been happier in my damn life.

Everything is going fucking perfect.

I opened my training gym two months ago. I've been teaching MMA to both kids and adults and I couldn't have asked for a better family of people to have at my gym as both trainers and students.

Eden and I moved in with each other just before I opened my gym and Alec was so excited I was going to be around more that he slept at the foot of our bed for a week straight and followed me around the house every chance he got.

We've been spending all the time in the world together that it honestly feels as if he's my own son. I love him as if he is. That's for sure.

Eden took Knight to court and set up child support arrangements and that's the only involvement he has in Alec's life now.

That's pretty fucking shitty on his part but Alec doesn't seem to mind now that he's with me every day and like I said before . . . I'm not going anywhere.

After shutting off the lights and closing down for the night, I hop into my truck and head over to Cale's.

Of course the whole crew is already here when I walk through the back fence.

Slade, Aspen and their newborn son Mason.

Hemy and Onyx with her swollen belly.

Cale, Riley and baby Haven.

Stone and Sage.

Styx and Meadow.

And *my* family: Eden and Alec.

They're all sitting around the huge table, waiting for my ass to arrive.

There's so much food out that you'd think we're expecting the whole neighborhood to show up.

Slade stands up and tosses a brat at me with a grin. "Sit down so we can eat, dickhead."

"Language!" Aspen scolds him. "You're gonna have to learn to get that in check now."

Slade uncovers Mason's ears. "I covered his ears, babe. I'll take care of this little guy with my life." He kisses his baby on the forehead as if he's the most precious thing in this world. "I love this little guy more than my own life."

"You're a good father," Riley adds. "I'm so happy for the two of you. Even though you didn't tell us right away! But . . . I guess I forgive you."

Sage reaches over Stone to grab for the corn, but he bites her arm and hands it to her instead. "I got you, babe."

"Bite me again and I'll be sure to bite you later."

Onyx laughs and rubs her belly. "You should know by now that threatening to bite any of these men will do nothing but turn them on and excite them."

"I'm always excited," Hemy says with a grin. "Bite me and it's on against every surface in the house. Pregnant or not. You're gonna feel that bite."

I take my seat between Alec and Eden and cover Alec's ears. "Hey now. There's little ears here that understands somewhat. Let's not talk about banging all around the house. Not until we're away from the table at least."

Eden leans in and kisses my neck. "Thank you, babe. I was too far away to protect him from this crazy group."

"Ouch!" Meadow squeals as Styx bites her bottom lip with a

growl. "That was really hard!"

Styx rubs his thumb over her lip and then gently kisses it. "Sorry, babe. All this talk about biting has me wanting to be rough."

"Really guys?" Cale says while bouncing Haven up and down on his knee. "Can we ever get through dinner without someone being bitten or fondled? Just remember at some point these babies are growing up." He rubs the top of Alec's head. "And We have this little guy."

Alec laughs and bites into his hotdog as if he's just happy to be here with everyone.

We've been doing this once a month for the last six months and Alec loves being around everyone. He barely wants to leave once we get here so we have to wait for him to fall asleep so we can slip out without him noticing.

We're all a big family here and no one will ever let anyone hurt our family.

Alec jumps up and screams Hannah's name when her and Abe show up.

He somehow managed to weasel his way back into her life. But I'm good with it as long as he doesn't hurt her again. I'd hate to have to kick his ass after he's been working his ass off for me.

I take a bite of my steak, before leaning over to run my lips up Eden's neck, stopping below her ear. "I love you so damn much, baby. This—us being a family—makes me happier than I've ever been. I'm never going anywhere. You and Alec are my life. Never forget that."

She turns to me and grabs my face, pulling me in close so she can speak against my lips. "I know that, baby . . . Alec knows that. We love you more than life. We're a family and I would've have it any other way."

Eden and Alec have made my life complete in the last six

months and I promise to do everything in my power to keep them safe and protected.

I'd give my life just to keep them happy. This is what life is made of. Love, happiness and family. And mine is right here next to me . . .

Eden

My heart swells with joy when I walk into the living room to see Alec sleeping in Kash's arms, with his little arms wrapped tightly around Kash.

The position Kash is in looks uncomfortable, but he doesn't move anyway.

"Want me to take him to his room." I get ready reach for Alec, but Kash shakes his head. "Are you sure? You look uncomfortable."

"I'm good," he whispers. "Come here."

With a smile, I crawl onto the couch next to them and lean into Kash when he reaches one of his arms around to hold me.

"He just fell asleep. I don't want to wake him up." He looks down at Alec when he stirs in his arms. "He had a pretty crazy night."

I laugh quietly and close my eyes. "Yeah. He always does during our family cookouts. I should thank everyone for wearing him down. He's always so quiet after we get home."

Kash leans over and kisses the side of my head. "I'm always worn out after being around them too. I was hoping to spend some alone time with you tonight, but I think I like being right here, where I am. I feel most complete when I'm near the both of you."

My heart practically beats out of my chest from Kash's

words. "How do you do it?" I question.

He smiles against the side of my head. "Do what?"

"Manage to make me melt from your words. And make me believe that nothing else in this world matters to you other than us."

"Because it's the truth. You're everything to me, Eden. And I will keep on proving that to you for as long as I live. You and Alec both."

"I love you so much, Kash" I whisper.

"Love you more, baby. Always will."

Kash truly has no idea that there's no possible way he can love me more than I love him.

He came into mine and Alec's lives and made them complete. I honestly can't imagine him not being here. The thought kills me.

He's ours. Kash is everything we need and want and we're never letting him go. We're not going anywhere. That's a promise. . . .

THE END

acknowledgements

FIRST AND FOREMOST, I'D LIKE to say a big thank you to all of my loyal readers that have given me support over the last few years and have encouraged me to continue with my writing. Your words have all inspired me to do what I enjoy and love. Each and every one of you mean a lot to me and I wouldn't be where I am if it weren't for your support and kind words.

I'd also like to thank my beta readers. I love you ladies and appreciate you taking the time to read my words. And Lindsey and S Moose. Oh my goodness, ladies. You helped me more than you can ever know with all your notes! Thank you so much.

My amazingly, wonderful PA, Amy Preston Rogers. Her support has meant so much to me.

I'd like to thank another friend of mine, Clarise Tan from *CT Cover Creations* for creating my cover. You've been wonderful to work with and have helped me in so many ways.

Thank you to my boyfriend, friends and family for understanding my busy schedule and being there to support me through the hardest part. I know it's hard on everyone, and everyone's support means the world to me.

Last but not least, I'd like to thank all of the wonderful book bloggers that have taken the time to support my book and help spread the word. You all do so much for us authors and it is greatly appreciated. I have met so many friends on the way and you guys are never forgotten. You guys rock. Thank you!

about the author

VICTORIA ASHLEY GREW UP IN Rockford, IL and has had a passion for reading for as long as she can remember. After finding a reading app where it allowed readers to upload their own stories, she gave it a shot and writing became her passion.

She lives for a good romance book with tattooed bad boys that are just highly misunderstood and is not afraid to be caught crying during a good read. When she's not reading or writing about bad boys, you can find her watching her favorite shows such as Supernatural, Sons Of Anarchy, Game Of Thrones and The Walking Dead.

She is the author of Wake Up Call, This Regret, Slade, Hemy, Cale, Stone, Get Off On The Pain, Something For The Pain, Thrust, Royal Savage and is currently working on more works for 2016.

CONTACT HER AT:
www.victoriaashleyauthor.com
Facebook
Twitter: @VictoriaAauthor
Intstagram: VictoriaAshley.Author

books by victoria ashley

STAND ALONE BOOKS
WAKE UP CALL
THIS REGRET
THRUST

WALK OF SHAME SERIES
SLADE (WALK OF SHAME #1)
HEMY (WALK OF SHAME #2)
CALE (WALK OF SHAME #3)
STONE (WALK OF SHAME 2ND GENERATION #1)
STYX (WALK OF SHAME 2ND GENERATION #2)

PAIN SERIES
GET OFF ON THE PAIN
SOMETHING FOR THE PAIN

SAVAGE & INK SERIES
ROYAL SAVAGE (SAVAGE & INK #1)

CLUB RECKLESS SERIES
HARD & RECKLESS (CLUB RECKLESS #1)

BOOKS CO-WRITTEN WITH HILARY STORM
PAY FOR PLAY (ALPHACHAT.COM SERIES #1)
TWO CAN PLAY (ALPHACHAT.COM SERIES #2)

BOOKS CO-WRITTEN WITH JENIKA SNOW
DAMAGED LOCKE (LOCKE BROTHERS,1)

Made in the USA
Lexington, KY
18 June 2017